LOVE BY NUMBERS

Sienna Waters

Copyright © 2021 Sienna Waters

All rights reserved

The characters and events portrayed in this book are fictitious. Any similarity to real persons, living or dead, is coincidental and not intended by the author.

No part of this book may be reproduced, or stored in a retrieval system, or transmitted in any form or by any means, electronic, mechanical, photocopying, recording, or otherwise, without express written permission of the publisher.

All characters are 18 years of age or older unless otherwise specified.

Stay up to date with the latest news from Sienna Waters by signing up for my newsletter. Or follow me on Twitter or Facebook!

To N.–
The algorithm really does work!
xxx

CHAPTER ONE

The biggest night of her life.

The city slid by the window and Annabel settled back. It felt like the first time she'd sat down for months. Automatically, her eyes began to close.

"Oh, no you don't."

Her eyes snapped open again, long enough to glare at Billy.

"What?" he said. "You can't possibly sleep now. We're going live in two hours. And you want to sleep? Seriously?"

She snorted but straightened up a little anyway. The cab smelled of pine air freshener and sweat, hardly an intoxicating combination.

"I'm guessing you didn't bring a plus one," Billy said.

"You want to bet on that?"

Billy's grin lit up the cab and he brushed a hand through his blond curls. "It'd be the safest damn thing I've done all month if I did. Since when do you bring a date to anything?"

"I don't have time for that sort of thing."

Which was partly true.

Love By Numbers, or LBN as it was affectionately called, was about to launch out of beta. They'd worked years on this project. First just the two of them, then a growing army of coders and developers and assorted hangers-on. Her heart skipped a little at the thought of what they were doing, at the tiny flaws she knew were still in the app.

"Yo, calm down," Billy said. "We're all good. We don't have to be perfect. We can fix the infinitesimally tiny shit later. Right now, we gotta launch."

He was right, of course. But still, her fingers itched to get back to her keyboard. To make things really perfect. Except obviously they'd never be perfect. Not completely. Something she had to learn to accept. Or so said her therapist.

She reached out a hand to Billy. Her best friend. Her co-owner. Her partner in all things business. "Are you ready for this?"

Billy sniffed. "I've been ready for this for years, babe."

She almost felt like she had been too.

Five years ago, Billy had come to her with the idea of starting a dating app. Sex sells, had been his argument, and she'd bought it, eventually. But only when logic had been added into the mix. Only when a complicated and beautiful algorithm had been designed to make perfect matches. Only then had she been completely sold.

"We're gonna be big," Billy said, squeezing her hand. "We're gonna be huge. Just you wait."

Which would be good, obviously. Good because then she could get out of the city. Then she'd have offers from the West Coast, then she could really make her mark in the Valley, really get her name out there, really start to work on the big stuff, the cool stuff, the serious coding.

"Where's Cassie?" she asked suddenly.

She begrudgingly liked Billy's wife. She hadn't at first. She and Billy had been an item since the day she'd heard him pitch a ridiculous product called Skedaddle Skin in a business course her freshman year of college. Not a romantic item, but a kind of 'I've finally found someone who balances me out enough to make me able to do incredible things' kind of item.

So when Cassie had come on the scene, she'd been far from pleased.

But then Billy had appeared in full banana costume in their favorite bar one evening, fresh from promoting his Skedaddle Skin banana skin composting idea, and Annabel had rolled her eyes and caught Cassie doing the exact same thing. And a fragile bond had been built.

"She's meeting us there," Billy said now. Which was hardly surprising since they'd been at the LBN office until fifteen minutes ago. "And you seriously really didn't bring a date?"

Annabel shifted in her seat. "Since when have you known me bring a date to anything?" she echoed.

Better to go alone. Better to be her own boss and not have someone else to worry about.

"Um, since never. But this is a dating app, Annabel. Romance is our business. I'd have thought…" He sighed and didn't tell her what he thought after all.

"Exactly."

"Exactly what?"

"Romance is business. That's it. Bottom line."

"You're in this for the money?"

"Like you're not," she said. "Yes, I'm in it for the money. And I don't see why I should let the fact that we're launching a dating app have any influence on my private life."

"But—"

"No buts, Billy. And no blind dates either." Over the years Billy had tried to set her up with every single woman this side of the river. "I'm busy, I have a career to focus on, and I'm just not interested. Romance is money, nothing more, nothing less. Can I be any clearer?"

"Fine, fine. I just think it would have made a better impression, is all."

A better impression. At their launch party. Potentially the biggest night of her life so far. A night she would attend alone. Like she did pretty much everything when Billy wasn't around. For just a second she gazed out of the window, wondering what it would be like to have someone waiting there for her like Cassie waited for Billy.

Probably a pain in the ass, she thought. Somebody to complain that she was late or that she hadn't come home last night or that she hadn't grocery shopped for two weeks and the fridge was

5

empty.

"You're looking great," Billy said, attempting to change the subject and flatter her at the same time.

"Thanks." It kind of worked.

She knew the reputation that geeky women had, knew the stereotypes of women that worked in tech. And she did her damndest to be different. She took pride in her appearance and the way she dressed, and her current little black dress had cost a fortune. But she was a knock out in it, she knew that. With her dark red hair swept off her face, her make up carefully applied, her feet crammed into heels, she could make a definite impression all by herself.

"While we've got a minute," Billy started.

And she was worried that he was going to get touchy-feely. That this was going to turn into a tears and thanks for being there conversation. But Billy knew her better than that.

"I've been thinking about marketing."

She relaxed into her seat. "Yeah?"

"Yeah. We need to make an impact, do something different, you know? Make a splash."

"Go viral," she supplied. It hardly needed saying since going viral was the short term goal of any tech company these days. Do something, say something, film something that caught on online and your downloads and profits could sky-rocket overnight.

Billy scratched his head. "Yeah, viral. I mean, that's the long term goal, obviously."

"So, what's your grand plan then?"

"A competition."

She lifted her eyebrows at him. "A competition? That's your big marketing plan?"

"We've got to put our money where our mouth is," he said. "We're saying we've got the perfect algorithm, that our system can find you your soulmate, so we need to prove that. We select a matching couple and then we fund them to start dating, as long as we can post pics and videos on social media. Like a live trial."

She breathed out, considering it. It wasn't a bad idea. It wasn't revolutionary, but it was simple and as Billy said, it could go a way toward proving what they were claiming. She could see no harm in it.

"Sure."

"Cool. I haven't worked out the details yet, but I'll get on it tomorrow, get a press release out there once the hype of the launch has died down."

The cab was turning now and they were a block from where they needed to be. And her heart jumped.

This could be it. This could be the whale they'd been hunting, the first truly big success of their careers and Annabel found that her heart was beating harder than she liked and that her palms were sweating.

"It's all gonna be fine. Great. You'll see." Billy put his hand on her arm and she smiled at him gratefully.

"I, uh, I couldn't have done this without you," she said, fully aware of the fact that she was the one uncharacteristically descending into touchy-feely land.

"Psh. I'm just along for the ride, you're the brains of the operation," Billy said and she knew he was just trying to make her feel good.

"Fine, maybe I could have done it alone." She swallowed and definitely didn't let a lump settle in her throat. "But I wouldn't have wanted to."

For a moment they looked at each other and then the cab was slowing down and Billy's attention drifted to the window and his grin was lighting up the cab again.

"There's Cassie," he said, waving like a maniac.

Annabel paid off the driver as Billy scrambled out of the cab to greet his wife. And they hugged and Cassie took Billy's hand and started to lead him inside. And after a moment Annabel followed.

This really was the biggest night of her life.

So far, she added mentally.

The biggest night so far.

CHAPTER TWO

If she was careful, she could make it from her tiny bedroom all the way to the kitchen without opening her eyes. She stumbled slightly as she brushed against the doorframe, but otherwise made it unscathed.

"Jesus, you look like death warmed up."

Indy did open an eye now, just a crack, enough to see Lucinda sitting at the kitchen table with a cup of coffee in one hand and her tablet in the other.

"Bullshit, I'll be fine after some juice and an aspirin."

She made her way to the fridge, finding both things there, her drunk-self had left the aspirin right where she was going to need it. She grinned to herself, took a pill, and chugged down some juice. Sure enough, a second later she could completely open her eyes.

"You know, I don't know why you go out on work nights," Lucinda said, watching as Indy poured cereal into a bowl. "Don't you regret it? I mean I couldn't function for the day if I had a hangover."

"That's because you're in law school," Indy said, taking a seat at the table. "Fortunately, I work in a call center, which is less mentally demanding and therefore means I can kill a few brain cells if I like. I have plenty to spare."

Lucinda laughed. "Fair enough."

"Besides, you only live once."

"So I've heard. Mostly from you. I'm going to hazard a guess and say that the date wasn't a resounding success."

"Eh."

Lucinda sighed. "So what was wrong with this one?"

"His name was Brian."

Fingers tapping on the tabletop. Lucinda's patience were wearing thin. Indy knew she should just spit it out and tell the whole story, but it sounded petty in the bright light of morning. Last night it had made perfect sense.

"Fine," she sighed. "He said his name was Jordan, but it wasn't, it was Brian really."

"And what's wrong with that?"

"Well, can you hear yourself screaming out 'oh, Brian' in passion?" Indy said, raising an eyebrow. "Besides, if he lied about that, what else did he lie about?"

"Was it really a lie though? I mean, tons of people go by something other than their given name. Probably Jordan was his middle name or something."

"Ugh." Indy pushed a spoon into her cereal and milk nearly spilled over the edge of the bowl. "It just wasn't right, that's all. No spark."

"Yet there was spark enough that you could pick him up in a coffee shop."

"I was wrong, okay? It happens. Sometimes it just takes a little time to get to know someone."

Lucinda turned her eyes back to her tablet. "So who's tonight's date with then?"

Indy chewed and swallowed. "Who says I have a date tonight?"

"You have a date every night, Ind."

"Jealous much?" Lucinda laughed again and Indy's mood started to improve. This was helped by the fact that her headache was starting to fade away. "Sorry, that was bitchy."

"Yep," agreed Lucinda. "And I'm not jealous of your tireless hunt for love. I swear to you. Honestly, it seems a lot more trouble than it's worth."

"Finding love is too much trouble? Seriously?"

Lucinda put her tablet down. "No, not finding love. But finding love so that you can check an item off your bucket list, finding love before some arbitrary deadline, that sounds like far more trouble than I'm willing to go to."

"My thirtieth birthday isn't an arbitrary deadline," Indy said. Then she remembered something and pulled out her phone.

"Oh God," said Lucinda. "You checked an item off your list last night, didn't you? Do I even want to know what it was?"

Indy laughed as she opened up the app. "Nothing horrific, I promise. But I did kiss under a full moon at midnight. So there's that." She checked the appropriate box, then remembered something else. "Oh, but then Brian told me about kite-surfing which I totally have to try." She added a new line to the list.

"So you came out of last night even," said Lucinda. "And you didn't answer my question. Who's tonight's date with?"

"Evelyn," Indy said, putting her phone on the table. "And she's amazing. Really amazing."

Lucinda rolled her eyes and went back to her tablet.

Indy knew that Lucinda didn't always approve of her life choices. She also knew that she dated a lot. Really a lot. The problem was that everyone she met was amazing. Really amazing right up until they weren't amazing any more. Usually for some stupid little reason.

"You know, you might have more luck if you were willing to overlook the small stuff," Lucinda said now.

"You're too logical. Love doesn't work that way. It's... It's a feeling. A thing. I don't know."

"But you'll know it when you see it."

"Exactly," said Indy.

And she would. She was sure of that. She was absolutely certain that one day she'd just know. That was what she was waiting for. So far it hadn't happened, but hey, maybe Evelyn was the one she'd been waiting for.

"What are you going to do if you hit thirty and you haven't fallen in love?" asked Lucinda.

Indy put her spoon down.

She and Lucinda hadn't been friends for life. In fact, they'd never met until Indy answered an ad for a room two years ago. But sometimes it felt like they'd known each other forever. Lucinda was like the sister she'd never had, and an instant friendship had sprung up between them. It was easy to forget sometimes that they didn't know everything about each other.

"That's not an option."

"No, it's very much an option," Lucinda said. "And I just want to know what's going to happen. I mean, are you going to move to a nunnery? Should I be looking for a new flat-mate? Or am I running the risk of coming home to find you swinging from the light fitting in your room? What are the consequences here?"

Indy brushed her light blonde hair away from her face and thought. She'd honestly not considered the fact that she wouldn't find someone. Falling in love by the time she was thirty had been on her bucket list for as long as she could remember. And she still had another sixteen months. It wasn't like she had to find The One within the next week. So she shrugged.

"Well, you let me know when you've decided," Lucinda said, reaching for the coffee pot and pouring herself another cup.

Indy finished up her cereal. Lucinda's question had unsettled her. But it wasn't something she could realistically consider. People fell in love all the time, right? And she was going to be one of them. And if she wasn't, it wasn't going to be through lack of trying.

"Crap, I'm going to be late," she said, suddenly spying the clock on the microwave.

She ran back to her room, brushed her teeth, tied her hair back, and pulled on the first clothes she could find in the pile on her floor. A long skirt and a tight tank would have to do. She grabbed a sweatshirt on her way out the door. The air-con at the call center could get chilly.

Going back into the kitchen to get her keys she saw Lucinda still at the kitchen table. "No classes today?"

"Not until twelve," Lucinda grunted.

"Cool. Well, don't wait up."

"I never do," said Lucinda. Her eyes were glued to her tablet. "Hey, you're on LBN, right?"

"What?" asked Indy, searching the counters for her phone before finding it on the table exactly where she'd left it next to her empty cereal bowl.

"Love By Numbers, that new dating site, you're on it, right?"

"Sure," she said, pushing her phone into her purse.

She was on every dating site. Just in case. Because you never knew where love lurked. It might be your best friend's sister, it might be the guy opposite you on the subway, it might be the woman in front of you at the movies.

"They're running a competition," Lucinda says. "It sounds cool. Right up your street."

"Yeah?"

"Well, they're paying for you to go on a date with your soulmate," said Lucinda. "And since you're chronically broke and permanently searching for love, that sounds like something you'd be into."

"Now who's being bitchy?"

Lucinda pressed something on her tablet and then looked up and grinned. "You're right. But so am I. I texted you the article. Read it. Could be fun."

Indy rolled her eyes. "You're so supportive."

"Only because I love you," said Lucinda, getting up. She squashed Indy into a quick hug. "Go on, go get 'em tiger. Your phone calls await. And you never know, today might be your day."

Indy was smiling as she ran out the door. If there was one thing that she definitely was, it was optimistic. Every day was her day. She bounced down the building stairs and out into the sunshine.

And maybe Evelyn was going to be The One. She hugged the thought to herself as she made her way to the subway station.

CHAPTER THREE

Annabel was well aware of the fact that she was intimidating. Which was why most of the staff knocked on Billy's door, rather than hers. Something that she wasn't exactly upset about. The little problems, those she could delegate, it was the bigger stuff that she was worried about.

Not that she had all that much to worry about. Looking at the numbers now, it was clear to see that LBN had had a successful launch. Subscribers were signing up in droves and ad spend was steady and profits were starting to roll in.

It was an odd feeling.

Not to be successful, exactly. She'd expected that. From the moment she'd started working on the project she'd had that tickle at the back of her neck that told her they were onto something good. No, it was more the idea of having actually achieved something tangible. She'd always excelled. At school, at university, and now here. But this was the first time that she could see real profit. The kind of profit she could spend.

She sat back in her chair.

Just what was she going to spend her money on?

She had a decent apartment already. A solid wardrobe. She tried to think of something that she wanted, something that would be her first big purchase. And drew a blank.

She sighed.

She was also well aware of the fact that she wasn't exactly

the most interesting of people. Probably because she devoted all her time to work. Sometimes she thought that the only reason she and Billy got along so well was because they had work in common.

There was no time for anyone or anything else, was what she told herself. But the truth was that she never made time. Work made her happy. She saw no need to dilute that.

Now she wondered though. Perhaps it was time to... extend herself a little. To take up a hobby, say. Her only issue now was deciding what that hobby should be.

She was idly scrolling through the list of classes at her local YMCA when someone scratched on her door.

"Don't tell me. You've sold the company to the Russians."

"Chinese," Billy said, with a grin. "I didn't think you'd mind."

Annabel rolled her eyes. "What's up?" She noted the time on her screen and felt her stomach rumble. "Lunch?"

"I've got an advertising meeting," said Billy. "No can do."

"Well make it fast then. I'm starving."

She pushed her chair away from her desk and Billy came in and after a single moment of hesitation, closed the office door behind him. Annabel's eyebrows shot up. Billy was a big believer in the open door policy.

"Do we have a problem?" she asked.

Billy rubbed his nose and then sat. Every now and again she could see the older man that he'd become, the true adult that hid behind his young features. "Maybe," he said. "That sort of depends on you."

She sighed again. "Cut to the chase, Billy."

"The competition."

"I already said it was a fine idea. And didn't you send out the press release already?"

"I did, and it got some good buzz. This should be a winner," said Billy. "In fact, we've already drawn one half of the couple." He pulled out his phone and flicked around on it for a second. "Here, have a look."

Annabel stretched over her desk to take his phone and then

studied the screen. "Indigo?" she said, looking at the sharp features of the profile pic.

"That's right. Real name too, not just a screen name."

She narrowed her eyes. The woman had blonde hair so pale it was almost white, wavy in a way that suggested she didn't own a blow dryer. Her eyes were blue, nearly turquoise, and her face was heart-shaped, her wide smile generous and open.

"So what's the problem then?"

"We ran the match." Billy stopped and rubbed his nose again, a sure sign that he was uncomfortable with where this was going.

"You put the magical algorithm to work," said Annabel. "And what? You didn't find a match? It's going to happen sometimes. I mean, it's not like everyone in the world is signed up for the service, you know?"

"Oh no," Billy said. "We found a match. One match. A perfect match. Just like the algorithm is supposed to find."

"So what's the damn problem then?" Her stomach growled again and she was thinking about the pizza from the stand on the corner so she barely registered what Billy said the first time.

"The match was you."

"What?" Her eyes flicked to Billy's face, sure that he was joking. But he looked dead serious.

"Your info was in the system. Nearly everyone on staff has their info in the system if they're single," Billy said.

"You made us all sign up when you went for the second round of funding," said Annabel, remembering. Billy had wanted to get subscriber numbers as high as he could, not caring where people came from as long as they became LBN members.

"Right. And she matched with you."

Annabel's stomach flipped. Her mouth went dry. Suddenly she wasn't hungry anymore.

"Are you okay?" Billy asked. "Only, you've gone a funny color."

"The algorithm must have a flaw," she said, mind already starting to run through where the problem could be. "I must have made a mistake somewhere."

"Why?" asked Billy. "There's nothing—"

"Can you seriously see me dating someone called Indigo?"

He stalled, then shrugged. "I guess it wouldn't be my first guess. Though to be honest, I've never seen you date anyone."

"Then I've made a mistake somewhere."

Billy burst out laughing. "Seriously, Annabel? Just because you get matched with someone? You've never even met the woman. You have no idea whether or not you're a good match. You can't judge someone on their name alone."

"I can and I will. And I have no intention of meeting her."

Billy stopped laughing now. "Come on, this is for the company. You have to."

"I don't have to do anything," she said decisively. She stood up. "I'm not doing it. But I *am* going to lunch."

She walked out, leaving Billy staring after her.

PIZZA SAT in her stomach like a stone and she stared at her computer screen trying to concentrate and failing miserably.

Billy was honest. Far more honest than he really should be. It was one of his charms, one of the reasons why he was such a good businessman, he was trustworthy. And he refused to mislead or even misdirect customers or investors. She knew that. Ordinarily, she loved that.

Now though, she wasn't so sure. Because Billy wasn't going to be satisfied with her saying no. He was going to push the point. The competition had a winner, one chosen fairly and honestly, and he was going to refuse to back down. And they were going to fight.

She closed her eyes, seeing the woman's face in front of her. Indigo. What the hell kind of name was that?

She had no time for dating and she definitely didn't want to be part of this little farce. Her answer was no, and that was final.

So when Billy came back just before five and shut the door behind him again, she'd steeled herself for the fight.

"Give me a second, Annabel. Just listen. Okay?"

She closed her mouth and nodded. Fine, she could play things that way.

"What better way of proving that we can do what we say we can, what better way of proving that we believe in our product, than having one of our founders go on a date like this?" he said. "I've been thinking about it, and I think it's great. A real big thing, something that could—"

"Go viral," she finished for him. "I said no, Billy."

He looked at the floor and shook his head sadly and in that moment she knew that she was going to lose this fight.

"Why don't you do it, if it's so important?"

"I think Cassie might be a little pissed," he said, looking up. "Come on, Annabel. Please? For me?"

Why was it so hard to say no to him? But she knew.

Billy had worked until fifteen minutes before his wedding, had skipped his honeymoon to come back to LBN. He'd mortgaged his parents' house and devoted all his time to the company. The only reason he wasn't divorced already was that he'd somehow charmed Cassie into putting up with him sleeping in the office three nights a week. He'd worked just as hard as she had, harder even.

"It's for the company," he said now. "This could really make a difference, Annabel."

"I doubt it," she said, already feeling herself buckling.

"Trust me."

Whenever he said that she felt a tickle on her neck. Because trusting Billy was the best thing that had ever happened to her. Trusting Billy had led to every success they'd had so far.

"Fine."

"You mean it?" he said, face lighting up.

"One date."

"One date," he echoed. "No problem."

He practically danced out of her office and Annabel screwed her eyes shut already regretting that she'd agreed.

CHAPTER FOUR

The night air was cool and the moon was shining. The silvery light on Evelyn's skin was entrancing and Indy definitely noticed it. The same way that she noticed the deep chocolate brown eyes and those tempting lips. Those curves and the faint flowery scent of her.

"Maybe we could do this again some time?" Evelyn asked, with a tiny smile on those enticing lips.

"Maybe," said Indy, brain desperately rolling, wanting more than anything to get the hell out of there.

Evelyn was definitely attractive. No worries there. She was tall and smart and funny and she loved music and reading and really checked all the boxes. She was even financially stable, had a job, and still spoke to her parents. So much to love.

But.

There always had to be a but.

Traffic streamed past on the street but it was like she and Evelyn were encased in a bubble. Evelyn was stepping closer, just a scooch, just enough to let Indy know what was on her mind. Enough so that Indy only had to take a step herself and they'd meet in the middle and then...

She edged back.

"Is there something wrong?" Evelyn's face creased into a frown.

Indy took a breath. Not wrong exactly, more just... not right.

Evelyn had moved constantly during their date. Fingers shuffling through the sweetener packets on the table, tapping on the tabletop, leg bouncing up and down, lips blowing hair off her face. There had never been a single moment of stillness.

And sure, it was cute. At first. But how could she live with someone in constant movement?

Yes, okay, she knew it wasn't the best reason in the world not to want to see someone again. But it was also far from the worst. She just couldn't see this working out. And Evelyn deserved to know the truth. Or some of it at least.

"I, uh, I have to be honest, Evelyn," she said. Her voice was steady. It should be. She'd had enough practice doing this. "I really don't think we should do this again. I, uh, well, I'm just not feeling a spark there, you know?"

Evelyn cocked an eyebrow. "No spark?"

Indy shook her head and for a horrible instant thought that Evelyn might cry or yell or take it badly. Not that she'd led the woman on, not really. But then Evelyn grinned.

"Fair enough. I didn't feel it either." She paused and looked at Indy. "But does that mean you don't want to come back to mine? No spark doesn't necessarily mean no fun, does it?"

Indy laughed. It was more than she deserved. She shook her head. "It doesn't, I agree. But I'm really not that kind of girl, and that's not an excuse. You're beautiful, you're funny, you're smart, and you'll make somebody very happy. But I don't do one night stands."

Which was completely true. True enough that she'd been celibate for almost two years now. No lie. One night stands had always left her feeling empty, like she'd missed something, so she'd made a rule not to fall for them anymore. A rule that so far was working.

Evelyn shrugged. "Suit yourself." She took a step backward. "Call me if you change your mind?"

Indy grinned. "You'll be first in line," she said.

Evelyn was laughing as she walked away.

Indy turned and started her own way home. She'd had high

hopes for tonight, mostly because Evelyn was so beautiful, so attractive. But it hadn't worked and she had to reconcile herself to the fact that tonight was not her night. Every day might be her day, filled with enthusiasm and newness, but sometimes it felt like it was never her *night*. Never her time to be filled with love, wrapped in warm arms, sated and satisfied.

She started to hum softly. It's never my night. The words twirled around in her head. There was something there. Yes, definitely. She could see the chords now, feel them under her fingers. She'd get a song out of this.

She hurried her step, wanting to get home, to get her guitar in hand and get to work. The night wouldn't be a total failure. Not if she got a decent song out of it.

THE KITCHEN light was on.

"I thought you weren't waiting up?" Indy said, sticking her head around the door.

Lucinda snorted. "It's nine o'clock. I wouldn't call this waiting up. Anyway, I've got a torts exam tomorrow."

Indy came fully into the kitchen. "I'll put the coffee pot on then."

"So, how was Evelyn?"

"No go." She filled the machine with water and flicked the switch.

"Surprise, surprise."

"Meaning?"

"Meaning, you can't date someone for longer than a week, Ind. Seriously. You're a serial dater, that's what you are."

"So you think I'm a slut?" Indy's hand gripped a mug harder than she should have and she felt her fingers squeak against the surface.

"No," said Lucinda evenly. "And I wouldn't have a problem with it if you were. Your body, your choices, my dear. I said you're a serial dater, which you have to admit, you really are."

Indy sighed. "I'm just looking for the right person."

"Which you might find if you spent more than five minutes in someone's company before passing judgment on them."

"So now I'm judgmental too?"

Lucinda put her book down. "You know, I think I'm going to quit while I'm ahead here."

"Good idea."

Her irritation drained away as the coffee machine did its job. Lucinda hadn't meant to be mean, she knew that. So when the coffee was finally done, she slid a cup over.

"Truce?"

Lucinda lifted her eyes and grinned. "Truce. So who's tomorrow night's date with?"

Indy bared her teeth and growled until Lucinda laughed. "No one. I have a rare night off. Actually, I'm going to be playing at that new coffee shop next to the grocery store."

"Really? Sweet. I'll try to drop by."

Lucinda was nothing if not supportive about her playing, even if she wasn't always totally behind the whole dating thing. "Thanks."

As Lucinda's eyes went back to her book, Indy pulled out her phone. She'd check her emails and then go to her room. That way she could fiddle with her guitar without disturbing Lucinda's studies. She slid through a bunch of junk mail until she got to something that looked important.

"Jesus."

She pulled out a seat and collapsed into it.

"Mmm?" asked Lucinda, buried in what she was reading.

"That competition? The one you sent me?"

"Huh?"

"The dating thing, the Love By Numbers one."

"Oh, yeah. What about it?"

"I won it."

Lucinda did look up again now. Then she frowned. "You know, something that I don't understand is that if you're already on the app, haven't you already found your soulmate? I mean, that's what they promise, right?"

Indy scoffed. "That's not how these things work. There's a free version and a paid version. If you've got the free version then you just add yourself and hope that someone finds you. If you pay then you get to see your match and their contact info."

"And you've got the free version."

"Yes."

"Wouldn't you be more successful with the paid version?"

"Wouldn't you prefer that I spend my money on little things? Like paying rent? And food?"

"Fair point," Lucinda conceded. "So, you won? Seriously?"

"Really, seriously." She scanned through the email again, heart beating like a drum. "This could really be it. Like, this could be The One, Luce."

"Or it could just be another date."

"Oh, ye of little faith. LBN promises that they have the most accurate algorithm on the market. They find soulmates, not dates. This is it, Luce. Really, truly."

Her eyes were suddenly filled with tears but she was grinning so wide that her face hurt and her pulse was pounding and her palms were sweating and this really could be it. Her search could be over at last.

Lucinda was watching her, face carefully neutral. Which was fine. Lucinda was no romantic. She didn't have to believe. Only Indy herself needed to believe. And believe she did. She always had. That movie moment when eyes met for the first time, when the music swelled, when the audience held their breath. She'd always known that she was going to have one of those moments of her very own.

She was furiously blinking away her happy tears when Lucinda spoke again.

"So who's it with?"

"What?"

"Your date," Lucinda said patiently. "Who's it with?"

Crap. She hadn't thought that far ahead. She went through the email again, more carefully this time. There were plenty of instructions, plenty of terms and conditions, and a couple of attachments that she needed to sign and send back.

But no name.

No picture.

No hint about her soulmate whatsoever.

"I don't know," she said finally.

Lucinda shook her head and went back to her book. "You be careful out there," she muttered.

And Indy read through the email just one more time. But there was still no clue.

CHAPTER FIVE

"I can't believe that I'm doing this."

"Calm down, it's just a drink."

There was that, at least. She'd persuaded Billy to downgrade the whole thing into a quick drink with whoever this Indigo hippie turned out to be. She wasn't about to waste an entire evening doing what amounted to promo shots for the app.

"I still can't believe I'm doing it."

The bar was quiet enough, she supposed. Probably because she'd insisted that this whole thing took place at six sharp, long before anyone would think of being out after work. Plus, the place was dark enough that she just might get away without being instantly noticeable or recognizable. There was only so far that she was willing to go.

"So Lars and Laura will be snapping pictures and handling the social media side of things," Billy said, gesturing over to the two blondes sitting in a corner, heads bent over their phones. "You don't need to do anything. The interns will take care of everything. All you need to do is have a drink and have fun."

"As if," snorted Annabel.

Billy cocked his head to one side. "Why don't you have a little faith in yourself?"

"What on earth do you mean?"

"I mean that you should have faith in yourself. This algorithm was your work, so why don't you believe that it can function as you designed it to do? You could be about to meet the woman that you're destined to spend the rest of your life with."

"Bullshit," Annabel said. "You can't possibly believe something like that. The algorithm is designed to closely match the listed preferences of subscribers, no more, no less. People like those that are similar to themselves. It's simple psychology. It has zero to do with romance and nothing at all to do with soulmates. You were the one that added that to the marketing plan, not me."

Billy sipped from his glass of water. "Okay then, why don't you believe that you've been matched with someone that might share similar interests to you? Whatever you think your algorithm does, you should at least think that it's successful."

"Because there are flaws in everything," she said. "I'm only human, after all."

Billy sighed. "Would it be such a bad thing to meet someone that you liked?"

She sighed right back at him. Billy, for all his wonderfulness in business, could be far too much of a romantic for her liking. "Just because you've got Cassie doesn't mean that everyone in the world needs to live your life."

"You're not lonely? You don't want to find someone who loves you? Someone you can love back? Someone to, I don't know, sit next to you at the movies? Sit opposite you at dinner?"

"I prefer going to the movies alone. That way no one asks stupid questions or steals my popcorn."

"Annabel, come on. You know what I mean."

"I don't have time for love and, frankly, I just don't think I'm built for it. It's not me." Billy looked at her so sadly that she patted his hand. "And it's not something that I particularly regret. I've got more important things to do than fall in love."

"Like what?"

"Like designing and running a best-selling app that will make millions and open doors for me to move to the Valley and get involved in some serious coding."

Another sigh. "Fine. Fine. Whatever. Just... Just do your best tonight, okay?"

"I swear."

"No yelling, no walking out, just play nice and have your pictures taken and promote the app."

"Done."

"Then I'm out of here. The last thing I want to do is distract you."

He left and she picked up her water wondering if she dared just leave. She knew she couldn't. Not when Billy had sacrificed so much for their business. It wasn't like he was asking a lot in return, was it? And this was for her benefit as well. It was to everyone's benefit that the app succeeded.

She shot a glance at Lars and Laura, still engrossed in their phones. Blonde and tiny and nearly identical she refused to believe they weren't related, though Billy insisted that they weren't.

There was the sound of a throat clearing.

Annabel turned.

Indigo was taller than she'd expected from her picture. Her hair was looped back into a messy bun. Jeans and a tank top did little to hide her figure, curvaceous and full, a waist that cried out to be held. Blue eyes crinkled as she smiled and Annabel's heart sped up just a little. Enough to remind her that she was there that this was happening that she had to go through with it now.

There was a faint smell of coconut.

There was a tiny, shiny patch of skin between Indigo's breasts.

There was a dimple in her right cheek.

The throat cleared again and Annabel snapped back to the moment. She held out her hand. "Annabel Taylor," she said.

* * *

The woman was not at all what she'd pictured. It wasn't that she wasn't attractive, she truly was. Dark red hair was pulled back and up, revealing sharp cheekbones and full lips. Her eyes were a navy blue that was almost black in the dim light. She was slim, but the cut of her blouse promised full breasts.

It was more... the attitude perhaps.

She was dressed in a suit, that probably didn't help. Indigo had never owned a suit herself, let alone something as swanky as the charcoal grey number molded around the woman in front of her. And her handshake, it was all business, tight and firm.

There was no pulse-racing, no spark, no connection as they touched. And Indy's heart sank. So Lucinda had been right. This was just another in a long string of dates. Nothing special, nothing remarkable. She contained a sigh. She had to try though. She was getting a *free* date, wasn't she?

"Annabel?" she said with a smile. "So is that Anne, or Bel, or Bella maybe?"

"Annabel. No nicknames."

The come back was immediate and sharp and she couldn't help feeling like she'd been reprimanded. "Oh, yes, sure, fine, sorry."

"There's no need to apologize. You did nothing wrong, it was an innocent question." The woman stared up at her for a second and she felt herself being examined. "Are you going to sit down?"

Indy took a deep breath before she pulled out a chair and sat. Her legs were shaking and her stomach was starting to feel funny. Stress. It happened like that sometimes before she got on stage to play.

"So, I'm sure you know who I am," Annabel said. "Which means we can talk about you. Would you like a drink?"

Indy nodded and Annabel gestured at the bartender. She leaned in closer, trying to place Annabel's face, then gave up. "Uh, sorry but um, I really don't know who you are."

"Billy didn't tell you? For God's sake."

"Billy?"

Annabel stared at her long and hard, then shook her head as if dismissing whatever she'd been about to rant about. Instead she took a breath and said in an impossibly patient voice: "Billy as in

William Elliot, the co-founder of LBN. And Annabel Taylor as in the other co-founder of LBN."

Indy's heart started beating normally again. For God's sake. Annabel was the boss. Okay. There was still a chance that this could really work. So maybe her date wasn't even here yet. Or maybe her date was the young blonde sitting over in the corner on her phone being looked after by another young blonde. Maybe, she thought, maybe they were both her dates. A man and a woman. How perfect would that be? Maybe this algorithm really was magical.

"Right," she said, smiling politely as a waiter put down a glass of water that she ordered in front of her. "So what do you want to know?"

The blonde man in the corner got up and came a little closer, flashing his phone and angling it. Taking pictures, Indy assumed. So he definitely worked for LBN. He was probably getting establishing shots, something to put up on Insta or Snap. She smiled and sat up straighter trying to look her best whilst not actually looking at the camera.

Annabel shrugged. "Whatever you feel like telling me. Where do you work, for example?"

"Uh, a call center. Is that going to be important?"

Annabel scowled at her. "How on earth should I know?"

Indy swallowed some of her cold water and put the glass down. "Um, do you think I could have a real drink? Something to kind of dull my nerves a little bit? Some Dutch courage?"

Annabel sighed but gestured at the bartender again. "Fine. Whatever you need. But it's not a good idea to drink on a date, you know. It's better to have your wits about you. You never know what might happen."

This was getting to be too much. She didn't want to blow what could be a golden opportunity. On the other hand, this Annabel woman was starting to annoy the crap out of her. She took another swallow of water before asking as politely as she could: "And when do you think my date will be getting here?"

Annabel scowled even further. "What are you talking about?

I'm already here."

The truth broke over her and Indy tried not to show a reaction. But she couldn't help flagging down the next waiter that came by.

"Whisky," she said. "Make it a double."

CHAPTER SIX

Annabel sat back in her chair. "Billy really didn't tell you anything, did he?"

Indigo shook her head. "Nope. Just to be here at this time. That's pretty much it." She paused for a second. "Well, to be fair, I signed a bunch of things and sent them to him, so there could have been some info there, I guess."

"You signed a bunch of things without reading them?" The thought made Annabel's stomach turn.

"Yeah. There, er, there really were a bunch of things. I had to go to work, so..."

A waiter put a drink down in front of Indigo and she picked it up immediately, drinking from it with her eyes closed in pleasure. Annabel's heart skipped a beat as the woman turned into the light, her fine profile lit up. Definitely attractive, the algorithm had that part right if nothing else.

"You had to go to work. At the call center." So much for matching career aspirations or financial goals. She'd need to look into that.

"Yep." Indigo put her glass down and pressed her lips together.

Somewhere in the background, she could hear Lars or Laura bumbling around, getting pictures, getting video. The noise reminded her that she probably needed to try a little harder here. She cleared her throat.

"Do you like working at a call center, Indigo?" There. That was good. Engage her in conversation about herself. What exactly did working in a call center entail? She had no idea.

"You can call me Indy, I mean, most people do. And what do you think?"

Annabel blinked. Not the response she was expecting. "Um, what do I think about you liking working in a call center?"

"Yes."

She opened her mouth, closed it again, then opened it again. There was no choice here but to be honest because she didn't have another answer. "I guess it's probably not the greatest?"

Indy laughed and took a sip of her drink. "Not really the greatest, no. It pays the bills though, gives me time to concentrate on other things. What about you? How do you like running a company?"

Annabel shrugged. "It's fine." Other things. Like hobbies maybe. Perhaps she could get a few ideas here. "What other things?"

Indy narrowed her eyes for a second, then caught up with the thread of the conversation. "Oh, other things. I, uh, I play guitar, write songs. Looking for my big break in the city, you know how it goes."

Annabel didn't, but she could guess. Starving artist, blah, blah, blah. Learning an instrument was not something that she planned on doing. So no help from Indy on the hobby front. There was another flurry of clicking as more pictures were taken, she remembered to smile.

For the company. This was all for the company.

"So do you have any hobbies? Anything you're interested in?" Come to think of it, she really should have studied Indy's profile a little better. Indy. She liked that. Liked it better than Indigo at any rate.

"I love reading. What about you?" Indy picked her drink up again and now it was more than half empty.

Reading? Christ, the last thing she'd read had been an instruction manual for her new washing machine. "Nope."

"Oh."

There was a lull as one of the blondes, Laura, Annabel thought, came in closer, zooming a phone toward them, obviously taking video.

"This is, um, kind of not relaxing," Indy said as Laura backed off.

"It's irritating as all hell," Annabel replied.

And Indy laughed. Annabel smirked. For a second there was one thing they could agree on. Annabel sighed. One thing. Not exactly enough to build a relationship on.

Indy was sitting quite calmly, her blue eyes taking in the room. There was nothing wrong with her, per se. She just wasn't who Annabel would have chosen for herself. Which meant that the algorithm had to be off in some way, a niggling problem that she needed to solve. Of course, the other problem was that she had no idea who she would have chosen for herself.

Not that that mattered.

If she was being completely honest, Indigo seemed like a nice woman. She was attractive. She didn't come across as a psycho serial killer. Annabel was fairly sure that she was nothing other than one of the million artists scraping by in the city. At some point she'd grow up, get a real job, get married and settle down. Just like they all did.

But one thing was stunningly clear.

This wasn't working out.

Not that she'd really expected it to, she supposed. Though maybe a tiny, tiny part of her had thought there could be a chance. Stupid really. Stupid because she didn't want anyone, let alone this girl.

"What are you thinking about?"

The question caught her by surprise. She looked up and found Indy's bright eyes on her. She thought about lying, about making polite conversation for another painful few minutes. But what was the point? It was painfully obvious that there was zero connection here and it was probably time that Indy learned the truth. That way she'd be able to get back to her real life and finding someone nice to settle down with.

Someone that didn't think washing machine manuals were fascinating reading. Someone who finished work before midnight. Someone who had interests and hobbies that weren't just, well, non-existent.

"Give me a second," she said, standing up.

She collared Lars and beckoned Laura over. "Thanks guys, you've done a great job."

Lars frowned. "Billy said—"

"I'm just as much your boss as Billy is. You've got pictures and video? Got all the social media stuff you need?"

They both nodded in sync.

"Great, then why don't you get out of here."

"But Billy—"

She bit her tongue. She was going to slap Billy. She swallowed down what she was about to say and instead said: "You know, every date could use a little privacy?"

A look of immediate understanding came over their faces and within seconds they were packing away their equipment. Satisfied, Annabel went back to the table.

"Sending the staff home?" Indy said.

It took a glance at her face to ensure that she was joking. A slight twinkle in her eye and a dimple in her cheek said that she was. Mostly. Annabel looked over, checking that there was no more filming happening and seeing Lars and Laura heading to the door. She let out a sigh and turned back to Indy.

"It's clear that you and I have nothing in common," she started.

"Was this a set up?"

Indy's question interrupted her train of thought. "What?"

"Was this a set up? I mean, you're the head of the company, there's obviously no real connection between us. Was this some kind of set up? Something to get some free publicity?"

"Not free," Annabel said, looking down at Indy's empty glass. "But, yes, I suppose it was a marketing thing, though not some kind of ploy. It was Billy's idea. My co-founder. He's... creative. And not always in the best way. The algorithm did match us though. I swear that's true."

"Huh. Maybe that algorithm isn't quite as good as you think it is then." Indy's face was harder now and she looked older.

The words stung. "The algorithm's only as good as the information I give it," Annabel said. She had to accept her own part in this, after all.

Indy sighed and looked at her empty glass as though contemplating another drink. "This was a bust."

"That's one way to put it," Annabel said carefully.

"Can't think of another." Indy pushed her glass away and for a second seemed almost sad. "I guess we can agree on some things though."

"Like what?"

"Like this was a stupid idea and neither one of us want it to happen again."

The weight of stress dropped from Annabel's shoulders. She was glad that Indy wasn't going to make a fuss about this. "No, I don't think it should happen again."

Indy nodded. She stood up and this time she was the one holding out her hand. Annabel eyed it for a moment, then stood herself, taking the hand.

"I'd say it's been nice meeting you, but…"

Annabel grimaced. "Right."

Indy reclaimed her hand. She took a long look at Annabel then she nodded. "Have a great life then, Annabel with no nicknames."

Annabel watched her leave, the sauntering swing of her hips as she walked, the way people looked at her and she didn't even notice.

Okay, okay, Indy was a beautiful woman. But they had nothing in common and this whole thing had been a disaster. She shuddered to think what would have happened if Indy had decided that she wanted to make a fuss about things, that she wanted to scream and shout in public. Annabel hoped that whatever Billy had made her sign prevented her from going to the press about this little screw up.

Still though. There was one good thing.
At least she'd never have to see Indigo again.

CHAPTER SEVEN

The day started with the alarm not going off and didn't get better from there. Indy managed to roll out of bed and dress in record time. She'd missed her bus and had to run, plus it was raining. Obviously. She was soaked before she'd even gone a block.

Her calls seemed to encompass only the obstinate, irritated or downright angry. And by the time she pulled off her head-set she was exhausted.

"You okay?" asked Amaria from the next cubicle.

"Awesome."

"Just that you look like you could punch someone. Not a good look on you, by the way."

Indy managed to grin. "Nah?"

"You're too skinny. I've been doing Krav Maga if you want to learn some moves?"

Indy looked at the girl who was just as skinny as she was and her grin turned real. "Sure, but not right now."

"Yeah, you should get home and take a bath with a big bottle of wine."

"Big bottle of vodka more likely," Indy said, pulling on her jacket.

She was out the door and back in the rain before she remembered the coffee shop gig. Crap. She considered canceling it, even just not showing up. But she couldn't. She'd promised to play and you never knew when your shot might come. Just like falling in love, right?

Her body got heavier at the thought.

Stupid date. Stupid competition. Stupid Annabel whatever-the-hell-her-last-name-was. Stupid love.

She hurried, striding through puddles and managed to make it home just in time to change, grab her guitar, and leave again. Back out into the rain.

THE COFFEE shop was warm and cozy at least. They'd set up a small stage and the waitress was kind in her introduction. And once the guitar strap was around her neck, Indy could disappear into the music.

It had always been like this, ever since she'd first picked up her father's guitar. She didn't have to think about it, didn't have to think about anything, she could just lose herself and play in perfect peace.

Unfortunately, the crowd was a bad one. Wet, tired and cranky after work, there was only a smattering of applause from them when she finished her set. She put a hat out on the stage, but didn't hold out much hope.

She was pushing through the crowded room to get herself a much needed herbal tea when a voice called out her name. She turned and saw Lucinda ensconced in an armchair, two mugs in front of her and an empty chair opposite her.

"Thank God."

She sank into the chair and accepted the mug from Lucinda. For a moment they were both quiet, Indy drinking in the warmth with her hands and closing her eyes.

"So, wanna tell me what's wrong then?" Lucinda said eventually. "Nice set, by the way."

"Thanks," said Indy. "And who said anything's wrong?"

"You look like you lost a buck and found a nickel," Lucinda said, picking up her coffee. "You might do better for tips if you smile on stage, just a thought."

"Ha ha. Thanks for the advice."

"So, what's going on?" Lucinda said, blowing on her cup of coffee.

"I—" Indy stopped, not knowing what to say.

What was wrong? Today wasn't her day. Except every day was her day, she prided herself on that. So what was wrong with today? She hadn't seen Lucinda when she got home last night, had told her nothing about the awful date, about the stupid competition. And now the world seemed a darker place, a heavier place and... And to her horror she started to cry.

"I, uh, I'm sorry," she managed to sob out.

"Jeez," said Lucinda, searching through her backpack and coming up with a crumpled package of tissues. "Here, here you go."

"Thanks," Indy mumbled, accepting them. She sniffed and then another sob broke loose, she just couldn't help it.

"You have to stop," Lucinda said, moving forward in her seat. "People are going to think that I've broken up with you and I'll look like a cheating bitch and then someone might slap me."

"How come you get to be the one who cheated?" Indy asked, waterily.

"Because you're the one crying," Lucinda said, sitting back again.

Indy sniffed, wiped her face on her sleeve, then nodded. "Distraction technique excellent. You've stopped my break down in its tracks. Thanks."

"Any time," Lucinda said. "Now, dare I ask what's going on? Or would that just provoke another break down?"

"I hope not, I'm almost out of tissues," Indy said, looking down at the package in her hands. Then she told Lucinda about her date with Annabel. Her date that wasn't a date.

By the time she was finished, she was sniffling again.

"But you didn't like her?" Lucinda asked.

"No. There was no connection. Definitely no spark."

"Then why the tears?"

"I—I don't know," Indy hiccuped.

Lucinda took a mouthful of coffee, then nodded. "Perhaps I do." She reached out and took Indy's hand. "You really thought this might be it, didn't you?"

Sadly, Indy nodded. "I guess. I just... I just thought that with the algorithm and everything that they promised that this was a real opportunity, that maybe finally I was going to find The One. Maybe I was going to fall in love."

"Just because it didn't work out doesn't mean that it won't work out next time."

Indy squeezed Lucinda's hand. "Thanks. But I think maybe you were right before. Maybe I'm just naïve and stupid about all this. Me and my silly bucket list. Who the hell cares when I fall in love? Or even if I fall in love? I should just give all this up and get rid of the damn list. It's more trouble than it's worth, you were right."

"No."

Indy raised an eyebrow.

"No," Lucinda said again. "Don't you dare give up. I know I give you shit, and maybe sometimes I shouldn't. But your belief, your naivety, your sweetness, they're the nicest things about you. They make you stand out. They make you different from every other cynical asshole that lives in the city. Don't change, Indy. Not because of one stupid date that wasn't even a date."

"Then what should I do?" Indy asked. Because she was exhausted now. She was tired of being bright and cheerful and optimistic, it could be so draining sometimes.

"Why don't you take a break?"

"A break?"

"Yeah. Take a break from dating. Say, I don't know, three months or so. Time to find yourself, to rest yourself, and then throw yourself back into the fray."

A break. It wasn't a bad idea. It wasn't a bad idea at all. She could take some time for herself. Work on some more songs, play more gigs, work on her career rather than her heart for a while. Lucinda was smart, therefore following her advice had to be smart, right?

"Okay," she said, just as someone tapped her on the shoulder. "Excuse me?"

"Can I help?" A middle aged man was standing beside her, shirt unbuttoned one button too far and hairline receding. At least he was self-aware enough to shave his head down to grey stubble.

"I was just wondering if you had a card or something I could take?" She must have looked confused because he added: "I heard you play."

"Ah, yes, right, sure." She reached into her guitar case and pulled out a card.

"Thanks," he said, lingering just a little too long. But when Indy said nothing more, he walked away.

"Well done," Lucinda said.

"For what?"

"For avoiding your first date," Lucinda grinned. "He was angling, definitely. And you blanked him. So nice job. Now just do that for three more months, clear your head, and you'll be good to go."

Indy stared after the guy. She hadn't had the feeling that he was after a date. But then she couldn't think why else he'd approached her for a card. He'd probably just lost his nerve and he'd call later when she was alone. And she would turn him down, because she was definitely going through with Lucinda's plan. No dating. Three months.

"Isn't there a box you need to check off on that bucket list of yours?" Lucinda said.

"Like what?"

"I don't know. A 'no dating' box, or a 'almost give up on the list' box, or, um, a 'get advice from a sage older woman' box?"

"You're like three weeks older than me."

"Still counts," Lucinda said. "How about I take you home and warm up some pasta? You can take a bath and disappear into a book and get an early night?"

Indy nodded, getting up. "I don't deserve you."

"You don't," Lucinda said, getting up and reaching over to grab the hat from the stage. "You don't deserve this either."

Indy took the hat. All of four bucks. Fantastic. And here she was thinking her day couldn't get worse.

"Come on," Lucinda said. "I might be able to scrape up some red wine to go with that pasta."

"Now you're talking," Indy said, and she picked up her guitar to follow Lucinda.

But she felt eyes on her back as she was leaving. When she turned she saw that the man who'd taken her card was watching her. She shivered. She'd have no trouble turning him down, she thought. Watching her like that was just creepy.

CHAPTER EIGHT

She'd unhooked the whiteboard from the wall of her office and propped it up by the door, freeing up the entire wall. Then it had been simple to grab a projector from one of the meeting rooms and emblazon her code onto the white paint. Big letters, big numbers, big symbols.

Annabel leaned back in her desk chair and surveyed the lines on the wall.

Somewhere here was something that she'd missed, she just knew it.

As much as she didn't want to think about the previous night, she couldn't help it. Now at least she knew why people complained about dating, she supposed. It was a nightmare. A horrific, uncomfortable experience that left you feeling like a piece of meat at the butcher's shop. There was no chance in hell that she'd be doing that again.

However, her twenty minutes with the little hippy had done her a favor. It had brought to her attention just how off her code could be. In a way, she was even glad that Billy had forced her to go on the date. Now she had user experience, now she could improve their product, refine the algorithm, make LBN even more accurate and therefore even more popular.

Not that she was foolish enough to believe that an algorithm could predict love. It couldn't. At least not yet. But she did know that it could be more accurate. And the better she made it, the more money they'd make, and the better opportunities she'd get when she moved to the Valley.

She narrowed her eyes as she read through line after line of code. It helped to have it like this, in big letters on the wall, made it easier to read.

"Aha," she sat up, read over a line again, then shook her head and sat back. No, that wasn't it.

She was about half way through the job when there was a tremendous crash from behind her and the lights came on.

"What the hell?"

She swiveled her chair around to see Billy standing in the open doorway, the whiteboard at his feet.

"Annabel, what are you doing?"

"Surveying code."

"Ah. Okay." He glanced up at the wall and shrugged. "Alrighty. Whatever works for you. Listen, we need to talk."

"About what?"

He rubbed his nose and smiled at her. "Got time for a drink after work?"

She didn't miss the fact that he hadn't answered her question. But it had been weeks since the two of them had hung out alone. They'd both been devoting way too much time to LBN. So she smiled right back. "Sure thing."

A DRINK was already at the table for her. A weak gin and tonic made with slimline tonic and Tanqueray. Just how she liked it. Trust Billy. She slid into the booth opposite him.

"Long time, no see."

"Indeed," he said. He held up his glass to hers and chinked it against the rim. "Here's to a successful launch."

"A successful launch," she echoed.

It had used to be like this a lot. Her and Billy sitting in a darkened bar discussing strategy and making plans. But then the plans had started to ripen and Billy had got married and all of a sudden Annabel was spending more time alone than even she wanted. So she was in a mellow mood now, happy that she could spend a little time with Billy.

"So, you want the good news or the bad news?" Billy asked.

"There's bad news?"

"That sort of depends on who you ask," Billy said. He wrinkled his nose and sighed. "Alright. Let's start with the good." He pulled out his phone, clicked an icon and Annabel felt her own phone vibrate in her pocket. "Check that out."

Obediently, she opened her phone and found an email. An email with a handful of links in it. Carefully, she clicked on a Twitter link to find a picture of her and Indigo with the hashtag #IndyAnna.

"Look at the numbers," Billy said quietly.

She scanned to the bottom of the Tweet. A half-million likes. In one day. Jesus Christ.

"The other links are similar," Billy said. "TikTok, Insta, everything's trending #IndyAnna. You guys really struck a chord out there. Something about this is drawing people's attention in. Mostly, I think, because you're the owner, because you're risking your own heart and reputation. People are loving this."

She took a breath, eyes still on her phone, flicking through Instagram. "Good. That's what you wanted, right?"

"We've gained massive amounts of subscribers over the last twenty four hours. An eleven percent uptake, more than two thirds of which are premium memberships."

She did look up now. "Seriously?" That was huge, the numbers close to unbelievable.

Billy nodded.

"That's... that's incredible. And it's all because of this stupid date idea. Well done you."

But Billy wasn't smiling. If anything, he looked grim. "Here's the part you're not going to like."

Annabel was immediately on edge. Billy didn't get that serious often. She sat up straight. "What?"

"We need you to continue."

"Continue with what?"

"With this. With #IndyAnna."

She was speechless for a second, just staring at him. Then she swallowed and found her senses. "You know that it was a disaster, right? You know that we didn't get along at all. In fact, we could barely talk to each other."

"Lars did mention that they had to do some creative editing," Billy said carefully. "But they can continue to do careful editing, that's not a problem."

"Um, maybe I'm not being clear enough. We didn't like each other. We don't want to date."

"You spent all of twenty minutes with her."

"Are you questioning my judgment? Telling me that I don't even know whether I like someone or not?"

"No, Annabel, I'm just..." Billy sighed. "I knew that this wasn't going to be easy. I knew that you were going to take it badly. Listen, I get it. You didn't want to do this in the first place, but now you've already done it. And people like it, they like the two of you, they like the idea of the CEO of a dating company using their own company to find true love."

"Except I didn't find true love," interjected Annabel.

Billy rubbed his face with his hands. "Okay, what's the plan here, Annabel? What do you want out of this?"

"Out of what?"

"This business. This app. What we're doing right now. What's the plan always been?"

"To make money. Big money. Fuck you money. Enough money that we can go out and do whatever we want. You can buy a yacht and raise a dozen kids and I can head to Silicon Valley and work with the best of the best."

"Exactly. And this is how we do that."

"By propagating a lie?"

"By... manipulating people's perceptions of certain events."

Annabel crossed her arms. "You want me to continue to pretend to date this random woman because it makes people sign up for our dating platform."

For an instant she thought Billy was going to deny it, then he shrugged. "More or less."

"You, who are the most honest and open person I know." He shrugged again and she leaned toward him. "Billy? Really?"

"Sometimes you have to do things you don't necessarily like," he said. "And this is one of those times. I'd gladly switch places with you, Annabel, but that's impossible. All I'm asking is that you spend, say, one evening a week in the company of an attractive woman and that you let Lars and Laura take some film and pictures. That's all it really amounts to. Is that too much to ask?"

"Indigo would never agree to it." It felt weird saying that, strange to assume that she knew the woman well enough to speak for her. Yet she did think she was speaking the truth.

"This is about you right now," Billy said. "The company needs you. I need you. We'd be idiots not to ride this wave that we've created. We could double our value by the end of the quarter. We could be selling for billions by the end of the year. You could be on your way to California by next spring. Isn't that all we've worked for?"

"And if it doesn't work?" She was starting to bend, starting to be tempted by what Billy was saying.

"Then at least we tried, right?"

He smiled at her and she had to smile back. It was exactly what she'd said to him when he'd been worried about mortgaging his parents' house to back LBN. At least we tried.

"One night a week."

"One night," Billy agreed.

For the company. For the money. For her future. She could do this, right? Was it really such a hardship? She didn't need to kill anyone or work out until she threw up or eat kittens or anything especially terrible.

"For you."

"For me," Billy agreed.

She looked down at the table. "You know, Indigo really, really won't agree to this."

Billy put a finger under her chin and tilted her head up. "Then you'll have to persuade her."

Annabel snorted. "Me? Persuade her? I doubt it."

"You can be very charming when you want to be, you know. When you forget that you hate all people and you only love code."

"I don't hate all people. I don't hate you."

"I know. Let's do this, Annabel. Please. It's just for a while, a few weeks maybe."

She picked up her drink, drained it, put the empty glass down and sighed.

Then she nodded. "Fine."

Billy crowed with delight and ordered another round of drinks. But that didn't stop her worrying that she was doing the wrong thing. Or that Billy was acting strangely, out of character, asking her to lie like this. Still though, it was nice to get some alone time with him. And she had to admit that the thought of making millions wasn't exactly hurting her decision either.

CHAPTER NINE

The call came on a Monday morning. Technically, Indy wasn't supposed to answer personal calls at work. But she was on break and just happened to be in the dead zone close to the bathroom where she had reception and knew that her boss would never catch her.

"Indy."

"Indigo? This is Annabel Taylor."

For a heartbeat, Indy considered hanging up. Her fingers itched to do it. But then curiosity won out. Why on earth would Annabel be calling her?

"Yes?" she said cautiously.

"This is complicated, I was wondering if you'd meet me tonight."

Indy snorted. "What? No! Why should I?" As though she was willing to go through that experience again. Anyway, she wasn't dating. She'd gone an entire weekend without dating.

"Because I have a proposition that might interest you," Annabel said. "Something that could benefit both of us."

Against her will, Indy's curiosity expanded. "Like what?"

"Just meet me, please? I get that you might not want to see me again."

"That's putting it mildly."

"But this will be worth your while, I think. Ten minutes of your time. Meet me at that hot new sandwich place on the corner of Madison at six. Dinner's on LBN."

She didn't have time to say yes or no. Annabel hung up, either fully confident that Indy was going to show, or nervous enough that she didn't want to deal with more conversation.

Indy leaned back against the cool corridor wall.

Now what was all this about?

Annabel was damn right that she really didn't want to see the woman again. On the other hand, it was ten minutes. Ten minutes and an interesting proposition. Which could mean anything. Well, anything except a date, since the one thing that was clear was that they had no connection at all.

She stood up. She needed to get back to work. She'd decide later, she figured, based on how she felt when she finished at the call center. If she was hungry, she'd go. If not, well, Annabel would live, it wasn't like she'd actually agreed or anything.

THE SANDWICH place was busy. Not crazy busy, it was only six, but busy enough that Indy could see it was popular. Glancing around as she walked in, she couldn't see any sign of Annabel. So she got in line and ordered herself a Reuben on rye, no pickle. Her stomach was grumbling and she figured that she might as well give Annabel something to pay for when she eventually got there.

She was waiting for her number to be called, leaning up against a tall table, when Annabel walked through the door.

She was still in a suit, a jaunty black number this time, with a cream shirt unbuttoned just far enough. Her hair was tied back, her cheekbones could cut glass, and if Indy didn't know better she'd be making a bee-line for her. She snorted to herself. Attractive women were ten a penny. Looks weren't the problem. Finding someone whose personality she liked was the problem. And there was something that Annabel definitely didn't offer.

They exchanged glances, Annabel nodded at the growing line of people, Indy held up her ticket and then Annabel got into line just as Indy's number was being called.

She was a quarter way through her sandwich when Annabel appeared on the other side of the table. It was delicious, the dressing dripping down the sides of her hands and she kind of wished she'd got more napkins.

"Here," Annabel said, pushing a pile of napkins toward her.

"Thanks," said Indy, swallowing hurriedly.

"Good sandwich?"

"Uh, yeah. Great." Maybe Annabel was actually going to be nice and normal this time. She scouted the dining room but didn't see any pale blonde heads. The photographers weren't here then. Well, she hadn't exactly been expecting a do-over of the date.

"Are you on social media?"

The question was unexpected and Indy raised her eyebrows. "Um, no. Well, yes, I am, but I never check it. Too much negativity and anyway, I'm generally too busy."

Annabel nodded. "I thought as much." She pulled out her phone, switched it on, then turned the screen toward Indy.

Indy squinted at it then drew back. "That's me. And you."

"#IndyAnna," Annabel said.

"Ha, that's clever. I like it." Then she realized what she'd said and wiped the grin off her face. "I mean I like how clever it is, not anything else, I mean, I don't like what it implies and all…"

"Calm down," Annabel said. Her long fingers darted over the phone screen, erasing the image. Her nails were neat and short, polished but not colored. "It is clever. And it's what I wanted to talk to you about."

"Go on then. You wanted ten minutes of my time and I'm almost half-done with this sandwich, so you'd better say your piece." She took another huge bite of sandwich to keep her mouth busy and stop herself saying anything dumb.

Annabel cleared her throat, obviously she was nervous about something. "The thing is, this, you and I, the date we had, it's, um, it's become very popular online. Of course, that was the idea. The competition was designed to make people sign up for LBN. But it's been more successful than we'd imagined."

Indy put her sandwich down. "You mean I'm famous?"

"We're famous. Marginally so," corrected Annabel.

"Cool."

"And, well, the company, me included, I suppose, think that we should ride this wave."

Indy's eyes narrowed as she took this in, then widened as she realized what Annabel was actually saying. "Wait, you think that you and I should, what, date?"

"Pretend to date," Annabel said. "And I understand. My reaction was the same. But we're trending, people want more of this story, and in the meantime, LBN is getting more and more subscribers. It wouldn't be a huge commitment, just one night a week or so."

Annabel's eyes were navy blue, a color that Indy had never seen on anyone else before. It was a beautiful shade. Annabel was beautiful. She was also hard to talk to and bossy. Indy shook her head. "No. I'm not dating right now."

"I'm not asking you to really date. It would be fake. All of it. Just a fake evening with some pictures and video taken. Not a huge commitment."

Indy scratched her nose and a number was called over the loudspeaker. Annabel looked down at her ticket, then disappeared, coming back a moment later with her sandwich.

"This is a big deal for you?" Indy said. "This kind of marketing, it's really helping your company?"

Annabel nodded, unwrapping the greaseproof paper around her meal.

"But your company's based on an algorithm that doesn't do what you promise," Indy pointed out. "It matched us, and we're no match at all."

"I'm working on it," Annabel said. "I agree that the app needs to get better at what it does, though it's never going to be perfect."

Indy looked at her sandwich thoughtfully. "So you get a successful company and free advertising and you make a bajillion dollars. What do I get out of this deal?"

"You're a musician, right? A song writer, you said? So, you get free publicity too. People know your face, know who you are. That can't hurt. Plus, obviously the company will pay for any kind of activity that we do, food we eat, that sort of thing."

Free publicity wasn't something that she could turn her nose up at. And yet...

"I want you to find me love."

Annabel looked up from her sandwich. "What? I thought you weren't dating."

"I'm not. Not for three months. Which is as long as I'll give this. And when the three months is up and you've improved your algorithm or app or whatever, then you have to help me find my real soulmate."

"So you'll do it?"

Annabel's face looked eager, younger somehow. One eyebrow was arched and a strand of dark red hair had come loose from its bun and sandwich dressing was dripping down her hand. Yet Indy still had reservations. Should she be doing this? Pretending to be someone, something she wasn't? It didn't seem right. But then, wasn't that what actors and models did all the time in advertisements?

She chewed her lip in indecision.

"What's on that sandwich?" she asked suddenly.

Annabel frowned. "Reuben on rye with no pickle."

Indy laughed. A sign if ever she could have asked for one. Maybe she and Annabel agreed on more than they might think. Maybe this might even be fun, in a weird kind of way. And maybe she still had a chance to tick 'fall in love before you're thirty' off her bucket list. "Okay, okay."

"Okay you'll do this?"

"I'll do it. Three months max. And you find me my soulmate when we're through."

Annabel shrugged. "Whatever you say. You can have free premium membership to LBN."

And a spark of contrariness lit in Indy's stomach. "No, well, yes, I suppose. But you're responsible for this. Whatever the app says. It's you that has to find my soulmate, no matter how you do it. I'm not taking chances on that algorithm not actually working again."

Annabel eyed her for a second then shrugged again. She held out a hand, withdrew it and wiped off the Russian dressing, then held it out again. Indy took it. "Deal."

"Deal," Indy echoed.

CHAPTER TEN

Once every two weeks, Annabel finished work at five o'clock and went straight to class. Her own class, that was. Women in Tech was a program started by one of her heroes, Annie Harland, and she went out of her way to ensure that she taught one coding class per semester. It was the least she could do.

Growing up in a world surrounded by men, with very little feminine influence, had certainly made her career choice harder, and she was a firm believer in making the world a better place for the women that came after her.

Which was all very well and good.

The flip side of all this was that the adult education center she taught at was literally across the street from Billy and Cassie's apartment. Which had led Cassie to determine teaching nights were also 'dinner with the old married couple nights.'

Wine bottle in hand, Annabel knocked on the door. She was tired, she had code to work on, and she really didn't feel like chatting and making nice. Billy said this was her chance to be a real human for a change, but in Annabel's opinion there was a lot of small talk that accomplished nothing. Mostly because Cassie forbade all talk of LBN or anything work related in the apartment.

"Come in, come in. Billy's running late as usual," Cassie said, opening the door and ushering her inside.

"I bought wine," said Annabel, holding out the bottle.

"So you did."

Cassie took the bottle, nipped into the kitchen, and in the amount of time it took Annabel to get settled on the couch had brought back a wine glass for her. Cassie, Annabel noted, was drinking something that looked an awful lot like sparkling water.

"So, tell me everything," Cassie said, sitting down.

Annabel frowned. "Everything about what?"

"About Indy, about dating, about the new big thing," said Cassie. Her curls bobbed as she spoke and her cheeks had a natural flush. She looked like a farm girl, all nature and no makeup. In fact, she was a clinical psychologist, something that made Annabel nervous every time they were in a room alone together. Like right now.

"Yeah, you know that's not real, right?"

Cassie sighed. "Billy told me. But come on, there wasn't anything there?"

"Nothing," Annabel said firmly. "And there's not going to be. It's all fake for the cameras."

"You could see it as practice." Cassie crossed her legs. "Practice for when you start dating again."

"Who said anything about me dating?" She was getting drawn into a conversation she didn't really want to have. Which was the danger of being alone with Cassie. She was very, very good at her job.

"You don't want to date?"

"I don't have time to date."

"That's an excuse. If you wanted to do it, you'd make time for it. So I repeat my original question, you don't want to date?"

"Nope."

Cassie's dark eyes gleamed. "Why don't you take a moment to think about that answer?"

It was an order, not really a question. Annabel sighed. She did like Cassie, mostly. They shared Billy, they had the same sensibilities when it came to Billy's wilder ideas. More than that, Annabel had found that she could sometimes open up to Cassie, share things that maybe she wouldn't share with someone else. Like this, for example. She wasn't about to discuss dating with Billy.

Given that Cassie wouldn't allow LBN talk in the apartment though, she didn't seem to hold herself to the same standard. And it was easier to go along with her when she was in full on therapist mode. At least until Billy came home.

Did she want to date? No. That was her gut reaction. And she didn't really think she needed a reason for it.

"Still no," she said.

"Why not?"

Annabel screwed up her mouth in thought, then shrugged. "I'm better off alone."

"You're an only child, aren't you?"

"Yes."

"Were you always happier alone?"

She thought back to long afternoons spent wandering in the mountains by herself, to the dinners eaten in front of the TV because her parents were working, to the sense of self she found when she was working in front of her computer.

"Yes."

"And the thought of someone coming into your life now makes you feel, what?"

"Disturbed," was the automatic response.

She thought about her beautiful apartment, how clean and neat it was, how perfect, how she knew where everything was. The thought of someone else being there, someone being in her private space made her feel slightly sick.

"Do you have any intimacy issues?"

Annabel blinked her eyes open and stared at Cassie who smiled sweetly back. She cleared her throat. "Er, no. I don't think so. I've, um, I've had lovers."

"Uh-huh," said Cassie. "So maybe this will be a good thing for you. Maybe you should see this as an opportunity to learn more about relationships, maybe re-evaluate your life goals."

"Seriously, Cass?"

Cassie grinned at her. "Seriously, Annabel." She sat forward in her chair and suddenly looked like less of a therapist and more of a friend. "Don't you get lonely?"

"I, uh, I, sometimes, I suppose. Doesn't everyone?" Which was true. Sometimes she felt lonely even when there were other people in the room.

"And during those brief relationships with lovers, you never felt any goodness? And kind of desire to have more?"

"Not really." She stopped. "Sometimes," she said, not really knowing why she was being honest except that this was Cassie and she'd probably find out at some point anyway. Annabel was half-convinced the woman could read her mind. "Sometimes I want more. Occasionally."

"Like when?" Cassie pushed.

"Like…" Honesty could be dangerous. "Like when I see the look on Billy's face when he sees you."

Cassie rolled her eyes. "Uh-huh."

"No, really. I've known Billy a long time. I've never seen him as happy as when he's with you. That's a big thing for him. He was always, well, um…"

"He was always a womanizer. I know," said Cassie. "And nice job deflecting. You've turned this conversation into one about Billy, rather than about you."

"I didn't mean to." Except she did.

"It's okay to want more," Cassie said. "And it's perfectly okay to change your mind about things. And to be open-minded about things. I think you see this thing with Indy as an obligation, something you have to do because my idiot husband asked you to."

"It is an obligation. It's for the company."

"But why shouldn't it be for you too?" said Cassie. "Maybe it's a test, just to see how well you do with relationships, to see if perhaps you might like one in the future, or if maybe you're still definite about being alone."

"I guess," Annabel said, she hadn't thought of things that way. And this was why being alone with Cassie was a scary prospect. She definitely had a way of making you think differently. Perhaps that's why Billy loved her. Speaking of Billy...

"Is Billy okay?"

"Sure, why?"

"It's just... This whole thing is unlike him. He's usually honest as the day is long and I wouldn't have thought he'd have pushed me into this fake dating thing at all."

Cassie took a sip of her water. "He's just worried about the company, I think. Just like you are. You both know how fast tech and fads move. You're popular right now but that doesn't mean you'll be popular a week from now."

And choosing the right time to sell, the time when the app was worth its most, was going to be tricky.

"I guess," Annabel said. But she wasn't convinced.

There was the sound of a key in the door.

"Speak of the devil," Cassie said. "He's here and I'd better get that casserole out of the oven before it burns."

She dashed into the kitchen just as Billy came in. She didn't wait for her customary kiss. Annabel was good at spotting patterns in things, good at observing. And Billy always kissed Cassie the second he walked into a room. Except for today.

"Hey there, how was class?"

"Just fine," she said, not getting up. "The office?"

"Not on fire, nothing looks like it's about to explode, so I thought it was safe enough to leave." He stole Annabel's glass from the table and took a sip of it. "Nice wine. You ready for tomorrow?"

"What's tomorrow?" she asked, expecting to be reminded of a financial meeting or a marketing meeting or something else pedestrian.

"Your second date."

"What?"

Billy grinned and ran his hand through his hair. "We can't sleep on this, Annabel, we've got to strike while the iron is hot. I've already talked to Lars and Laura. Just... go to the movies or something."

He handed her glass back and she took a drink. Great. Movie night. Okay, okay, she'd agreed to all this, and it was only once a week. But still. She had better things to do at the end of a long day than spend two hours sitting next to someone she had zero in common with.

"For the company," Billy whispered into her ear before taking her glass back and drinking.

She groaned. "Right. For the company."

CHAPTER ELEVEN

She couldn't help but be a little excited. Sure, this wasn't a real date but... But it was as close as she was going to get to a real date for three months and she hadn't exactly had a lot of excitement lately. Indy hurried her step a little as she approached the movie theater.

"Hi."

Annabel came out of nowhere and began to walk beside her. Indy smelled roses and something else, something muskier, deeper. It was a pleasant scent. Almost masculine but not quite.

"Hi."

They kept in step, heels striking the ground at the same time and Indy didn't quite know what to say, so she kept her mouth shut. Let Annabel do the talking for once, this was all her idea anyway. They made it half a block before Annabel finally found her voice.

"Are you, uh, looking forward to this?"

"The movie or the anti-date?" Indy asked before she could stop herself. She took a breath. "Sorry. Um, I don't know, to be honest. Are you?"

A man coming in the opposite direction veered toward them and Indy was forced to move closer to Annabel, their arms brushing as they walked. Indy shivered at the touch. It was weird being so close to the woman, and weirder still because she felt like she hadn't touched another human being for months except it had really only been a couple of days and how hard could it be to stay single and celibate for three months?

"I don't know," Annabel said.

At least she was being honest.

And that seemed to cover the conversational part of the evening, since Annabel didn't say anything else and Indy still didn't know what to say and kept on keeping her mouth shut. It was almost a relief to see the blonde heads of Lars and Laura waiting outside the theater.

"Hi," Indy said, almost shyly. She didn't know if she was actually supposed to speak to the two, but it seemed only polite.

"Hey," grinned Lars. "How's it going?"

"Um, good, I guess. I suppose I should congratulate you on all your great work. The world seems to think that #IndyAnna is a thing and that's all down to you."

"Down to me," interrupted Laura. "I do all the social media stuff. Lars takes the pictures." She stuck her tongue out at him and he laughed. "I supposed I could share the credit though."

"What do you need?" interrupted Annabel.

Laura shrugged. "Just... go to the movies. This worked so well last time because it wasn't scripted, so just do your thing. Ignore me and Lars, pretend we're not here."

"Right then," said Annabel.

She strode toward the theater and Indy skipped a step to keep up, and then was pleasantly surprised when Annabel held the door open for her.

"Smile for the camera," Annabel hissed at her, which rather detracted from the effect, but Indy did as she was told.

Everything seemed to be going well, weird but well, until they were standing in front of the electronic board displaying the evening's entertainment.

"We'll see this," Annabel said.

Indy looked where she was pointing. A dreary period piece in Rumanian with English subtitles. "Um, no?"

Annabel sighed, looking annoyed. "What do you want then?"

Indy ran her eyes down the list. "What about this?" A nice

rom-com, that should do them, light entertainment and something that kept with the theme of the evening.

She looked up just in time to catch Annabel rolling her eyes. "Not a chance."

"Okay," Indy said, keeping her temper. "You choose another one then."

"What's wrong with my original choice?"

"Guys, guys, could you look less, um... less angry?" Laura said, hurrying up to them.

Indy took a deep breath and then smiled at Annabel as widely as she could. "I'm not going to watch three hours of poverty and prostitution in a language I can't understand."

"There are subtitles," Annabel said, through her own wide grin.

"What the hell's wrong with my choice?"

"Nothing, if you don't mind your brain rotting into mush while you're watching it."

Indy took a step back and her smile dropped away. "You're really shit at this, you know? Like absolutely terrible at relating to other people."

"I—" began Annabel.

But Laura had appeared again. "Guys."

Annabel turned on her. "You know, for someone I'm supposed to be ignoring, you're very apparent. It's hard to pretend you're not even here if you pop up every five seconds. What exactly do you want?"

Indy took a step toward Laura, just in case she needed protecting. The woman must be used to Annabel and her moods though, because she did nothing other than smile.

"I really need this to look like a date, not like a prize fight," Laura said. "The sooner we can get our shots, the sooner we can all go home."

Indy took a deep breath, time to be a big girl. Was Annabel really this bad with people, or was she shy, or nervous maybe? It was hard to tell. She got the impression that the woman didn't make friends easily. But she could be wrong. It wasn't like she knew her well. But obviously someone needed to step up here.

"You know, we can go and see different movies," she said.

Laura's face lit up and even Annabel looked interested.

"Let's just do the photos and video here, then we'll both go see whatever we want, and get another couple of pictures when we're done," Indy continued.

Which was what they ended up doing. They played their roles, lined up for snacks, and after an awkward exchange of popcorn buckets and sodas, they went their separate ways.

A very accurate representation of the kind of relationship they had, Indy couldn't help but think, as she took herself off to her film.

IT WAS dark when she got home, but not quite late enough for Lucinda to be in bed.

"Want some cocoa?" Lucinda called from the kitchen.

"Sure," Indy said, coming in and ditching her keys on the counter. "You know, sometimes I really think you're from the nineteen fifties. Cocoa before bed and all."

"Don't pretend like you don't like it," Lucinda grinned. "How was your not-date?"

Indy shrugged. "Fine, I guess. I mean, we didn't date. We saw separate movies and everything. And you're being suspiciously supportive of all this."

"Am I?" Lucinda asked, eyebrow raised.

"I'd have expected you to be firmly against me seeing Annabel again."

"Well, it's not breaking the 'no dating for three months' rule," Lucinda said, pouring cocoa into a mug. "And actually, as dodgy as this whole thing sounds, I think it might be good for you."

"Okay, how exactly?" She accepted the cup.

Lucinda leaned against the kitchen counter. "Well, I think it's a good idea for you to spend more than one date with someone. Even if they're not real dates. Maybe it'll help you to see that everyone has flaws and that putting up with those flaws is part of life. Your problem is that you get one whiff of something less than perfect and you move on to the next person immediately."

"Not true," Indy said, though she knew it probably was. Strike that. Definitely was.

"We'll see," Lucinda said, picking up her own cocoa. "You might just learn something here, mark my words. And now it's time for me to hit the hay. Night."

"Hit the hay," Indy said. "I told you you were from the nineteen fifties."

"Night," Lucinda said again, disappearing to her room.

Indy sighed. She wasn't tired yet, the movies always left her more energized than when she went in. She pulled out her phone and checked her emails instead, before noticing a strange icon in the top corner of her phone. She stared at it for a second before realizing that it meant she had voicemail.

Voicemail? Really? Who the hell left voicemail these days?

She pressed the icon and turned the sound up until a man's voice echoed through the kitchen.

"This is Dan Rivers calling for Indigo Chambers."

Huh, so much for thinking it was a wrong number. But who the hell was Dan Rivers? She moved the phone closer to her ear, cocoa cup hot in her other hand.

"We met the other night after your set in the coffee shop, I asked for your card."

That explained that. Her stomach sank. He was going to ask her out, she was sure of it. Well, at least she didn't have to turn him down in person.

"If you could give me a call on…"

He rattled off his phone number. Maybe she did have to turn him down in person, or at least over the phone. It was only polite to call back, wasn't it?

"I'd like to discuss the possibility of representing you."

Slowly, very slowly, she put her cocoa mug down on the counter. Representing her. He was an agent. Dan Rivers was an agent. Her heart about stopped in her chest. A real agent, someone in the business, someone interested in what she did, in her songs, her music. Her hands were sweating and she didn't hear the end of the voicemail.

In her head she could see the entry on her bucket list. 'Get an agent'. And then the little check box after it. An entry she'd begun to think she'd never be able to tick off.

An agent.

She whooped in pure delight, happiness filling her to the brim.

"Are we being robbed?" Lucinda asked, popping her head around the door and rubbing her eyes.

"No," Indy said. "We're celebrating."

CHAPTER TWELVE

Annabel walked down the corridor, past the flashy wall graffiti that every start-up these days seemed to have, and stuck her head into Billy's office.

"Hey, I—"

She was half-way through her sentence when she realized he wasn't there. Odd. His jacket was hanging on the back of his chair and his door was open, but there was no sign of Billy. Huh. He had to be around somewhere.

She breezed past the meeting rooms, but they were all empty. He wasn't in the bull-pen, as the interns had nicknamed the large open office area in the center of their floor. So she resorted to knocking on doors of private offices, hoping to find him.

The third door she hit turned out to be Lars and Laura's, which she probably knew somewhere in the back of her head, but she didn't pay much attention to people who weren't directly connected to her. Though she supposed that now Lars and Laura were kind of connected to her.

"Seen Billy?"

They looked at each other, then at her, then shook their heads. She could see her own face on Lars's computer screen.

"Working on the stuff from the movie date?"

Another shared, pained look, then a nod this time.

Annabel frowned and slid entirely into the office, closing the door behind her.

It was a nice place, the windows large and there was more than enough room for the two desks. Not bad for a couple of glorified interns. There was a smell of cinnamon that reminded her vaguely of Christmas. It didn't escape her attention that neither Lars nor Laura had said a word to her so far.

She sighed.

They were key to this whole marketing ploy, and though she was sure Billy had them on a tight leash, it might be a good idea to play a little more nicely with them. Anyway, she needed info.

"Have you two noticed anything strange about Billy lately?"

Maybe she shouldn't be asking employees things like that, but they probably saw him more than she did. And she was getting inklings of something going down. Okay, Cassie said he was working hard and worried about the company. But LBN was doing better than it had ever done before. Billy should be ecstatic, not worried.

He'd asked her to play along with Indy, which was unlike him, though she could see his reasoning. And now he wasn't in his office, which again, was unlike him. Billy would live in his office if Cassie didn't occasionally pull him out of it.

So she waited while Lars and Laura shared yet another look. Really, they had to be related, didn't they? Twins maybe, didn't twins have some secret language that they communicated in?

"Um, maybe," Laura said cautiously.

Annabel's attention perked. "Like what?"

"Like... well, he's not around as much as he used to be. And sometimes his office door is open but he's not there. It looks like he's just, I don't know, gone to the bathroom or something, but then a half hour or an hour later, it's still like that. Like he's left the building maybe?"

Hmm. Interesting. Why would Billy leave the building? Why would Billy be secretive? Even with her? Maybe he was thinking about selling out. But then, why wouldn't he tell her? He could sell his share, certainly, they were fifty-fifty partners, but it would be a hell of a lot easier to sell the entire company.

And that had always been the plan. LBN was a teething ring,

something to practice their skills on. Make some cash and then move on to bigger things. Though the idea of working without Billy made her feel more than a little nervous.

"Okay, thanks," she said to Laura, trying to make it look like she didn't really care.

Lars cleared his throat and gave Laura a meaningful look and Laura glared at him and Annabel knew that she was missing something.

"What?"

She could see Laura take a deep breath.

"I won't bite," she said. "What is it?"

Laura screwed up her face for a second, then breathed out. "Okay, um, it's about the other night."

"Okay."

"We, um, well, if this is going to work we need to get a certain amount of footage. And, well, it's pretty difficult to get a fake social media date out of what amounted to an argument and two people going to see separate films."

Annabel narrowed her eyes, then looked over at Lars who was nodding in agreement. Crap. She'd thought that she actually might get away with putting minimum effort into this. Billy had said that Lars and Laura could cobble together fake dates from anything.

"I could, uh, try harder, I suppose," she said, wrong-footed because these were technically her employees and she wasn't totally sure how to treat them.

"It would be good if you guys could, um, touch sometimes, or at least smile at each other," Laura said, warming to her theme.

Annabel leaned against the side of Laura's desk. "You know this is fake, right?"

"It was pretty obvious from the start that you guys didn't really like each other," Laura said, flushing slightly. "But I think we all need this marketing campaign to work, and that might mean faking things a little harder."

It was on the tip of her tongue to say something sharp and walk out. After all, Laura was an employee. But even Annabel could see that wouldn't be helpful. And perhaps Laura could be of use here.

"What would you have done?" Annabel asked slowly. "In that situation, what would be the right thing to do?"

"Compromise," Lars said, turning his chair further towards them.

"Compromise?" Annabel asked. "But then both of us would be watching a movie we didn't want to see, and that's just illogical."

"It's how these things work," Lars said, smiling. "And if it's a real date you're excited to spend time with the other person anyway, so you don't really care."

"So I should have compromised," said Annabel. "Okay. I suppose I can do that. I just need to see Indigo as someone I'd make sacrifices for."

"That would help," Laura said. "But it's more than that. I think you come across, as well…"

"Intimidating?" Annabel supplied. She knew that and it didn't particularly bother her.

"Cold," said Lars. Laura shot him a warning look but he shrugged. "I'm sorry, Ms. Taylor, but it's better that you know the truth. If this is going to work then you need to know that you give off the impression of being cold and, well, you're very difficult to get along with."

"Unlike Billy," said Annabel, guessing at the comparison before it could be made.

"Well, yes," Laura said. She glanced again nervously at Lars.

"Calm down, I'm not going to fire you," said Annabel. "You're doing your jobs. You're right, it's in everyone's best interest that this go well and if that means I need to take on a certain amount of personal criticism, then I guess that's just how it is. So. Cold and hard to get along with. Huh."

She wanted this to be done. She wanted to make money. More than that though, she wanted to succeed in life and she was smart enough to know that the impression she made would impact her future job opportunities.

And she honestly hadn't realized. She'd known she was intimidating. But cold? Hard to get along with? She hadn't deliberately set out to be that way, it had just sort of... happened. She put aside the hurt she felt and focussed on the issue at hand. There's be time to cry in the bathroom later, she was no stranger to that.

"What do I need to do then, to come across better?"

"Smile more," Lars said immediately. "And in this context, touch more. Nothing inappropriate, just a hand on the arm or on the shoulder."

Fine, she could do that.

"And be less guarded," said Laura. "You have to give away more information. You have to want to tell her things, rather than her working like a dog to mine nuggets of information from you."

Annabel had a sudden image of Indy bathed in sweat, coal dust on her cheeks, and her lips twitched at the thought of it. "Okay, be more open, smile more, touch more."

"Just... act more like you're in love, or like you're falling in love," Laura said.

She said it as though anyone would understand what she meant, not knowing that Annabel had never fallen in love, had no idea what she was talking about.

"Alright, I'm on it," Annabel said. She was about to add a whole bunch of romantic movies to her watch-list. That should do the job, right? And there had to be stuff online about all of this. She could learn to fake a relationship better. More importantly, she had to learn how to make a better impression, otherwise no one other than Billy would want to work with her.

"Cool," Laura said, beaming at Lars who beamed right back. "Thanks. That'd really help."

"You're welcome," Annabel said.

She left their office, leaving the door open. It had been helpful and she could see more of Cassie's point now. She needed to work on her personal skills, not necessarily her dating skills, but how she related to other people. She didn't want to come across as cold. Who did?

It wasn't like she'd planned to be like this. But after isolating herself for so long, after learning to rely on herself for so long, she supposed it was the natural consequence. Well, she could change it. And she would. Indy would be her guinea pig and Annabel was going to charm her. Or at least attempt to make her like her. Or tolerate her. Hell, just to make her smile would be achievement enough.

She passed by Billy's open door again on her way back to her office.

He still wasn't there.

CHAPTER THIRTEEN

Back on track, that was both the way she was feeling and the title of the song that she'd been working on all afternoon and was humming as she walked into the bar.

Sometimes you had to make changes to see changes and that was obviously what was happening. Choosing not to focus on dating meant that she got career opportunities instead, the stars were smiling at her. Even the thought of a drink with Annabel couldn't dim her happiness. After what had happened at the movies she figured she'd be in and out in ten minutes. Plenty of time to go back and work on that song.

Annabel was sitting in a booth at the back of the bar, two glasses in front of her. Indy could see the shining blonde heads of the production twins, as she'd taken to calling them. She took a mental deep breath and then walked over, sliding into the seat. Best to get this over with, then she could get home.

"I got you a drink, I hope you don't mind," Annabel said. She slid a glass across. "It's whiskey. It's what you had last time, so I thought, um, actually, maybe I was being presumptuous, maybe you'd have preferred to choose your own drink."

"No," Indy said. "It's fine. I'm just surprised you allowed me a drink."

"*Allowed* you a drink?"

"You were the one that intimated drinking on dates was dangerous," Indy pointed out.

"It is, especially when you first meet people. You can't be too careful in the city." Annabel stopped abruptly and Indy got the sense that she was holding her tongue. "How was your day?"

"Working at the call center? Oh, excellent, as usual."

Annabel swallowed. "Um, this is a nice place."

Wow, she was scraping the bottom of the barrel with that one and Indy finally decided to take pity on her. For whatever reason, Annabel had apparently decided to be nice tonight. "It's cool here," she agreed. "And how was your day?"

"Long and busy, I've got some complicated coding stuff that I need to take care of and..." Annabel stopped again, clearing her throat. She smiled and her face lit up and looked completely different. "I'm not great at small talk. I haven't had much practice."

Indy laughed. "You're doing just fine."

"Am I? I feel like I'm in a bad movie. I watched a bunch of them yesterday. But then I did read online that the best way to make small talk was to ask the other person about themselves. So, tell me more about you."

Indy laughed again, and then laughed harder when she saw the offended look on Annabel's face. "Oh dear, I'm sorry, I'm not making this very easy on you, am I?" she said, as she wiped her eyes. "Alright, why don't we start over? My day was a pain in the ass, like work mostly is, but I've been working on a new song this afternoon and it's going pretty well."

"How do you write a song?" Annabel asked, leaning in. Her hand was on the table, dangerously close to Indy's.

Indy fought the urge to move her hand. "Um, it just sort of happens in my head. I can't really explain it."

"Okay," said Annabel. "I've got another question, and you don't have to answer it if you don't want to. But you said that you're not dating for three months. Why is that?"

Indy shrugged. "It was my room-mate's idea, to be honest. But it's a good one. I was dating a lot, getting too involved with too many people."

"Why?"

"Because... well, it's silly." And suddenly it did feel silly, sitting here in front of this woman who was obviously smart and knew what she was doing, who was successful and bright. But Annabel was arching an eyebrow and Indy gave in. "Because I've got a bucket list and because falling in love before I'm thirty is on that bucket list."

"A bucket list? Like a list of things you want to do before you die?" Indy had expected Annabel to laugh or be dismissive, but if anything, she looked interested, sipping at her drink slowly.

"Yes."

"And you've never been in love? I find that hard to believe."

Indy wasn't sure if that was a compliment or an insult, but she let it go, things were going better than she'd imagined and she didn't want to endanger that. "What about you? Have you fallen in love?"

"Psh, no. Never. I don't intend to either, I'm better off alone."

"I find that hard to believe," Indy echoed. The light was glancing off Annabel's cheekbones.

"And you turned to conversation to me, when it's supposed to be about you," Annabel said. "Tell me, what kind of music do you write?"

A dangerous question for a musician. For the next half an hour Indy talked about her music, her dreams, and every time she thought Annabel must be bored, the woman asked her another question and off it went again. Finally, Indy finished her drink, surprised to find her glass empty.

"What kind of music do you like?" she asked, feeling like she needed to direct the conversation Annabel's way.

"Oh, I can't say." Annabel paused and blushed. "It's embarrassing."

"Go on, tell me."

There was something nice about this Annabel. Something almost charming. Yes, she could be short and sharp and annoying. But maybe that was just because she was shy, Indy thought. Maybe she just needed someone to bring her out of her shell. She was already attractive, a little more confidence could go a long way.

"Eugh. Fine. I like seventies and eighties music, if I'm being honest. Something to sing along to."

Indy grinned. "You sing?"

"Alone. At home."

And the idea came to her fully formed. A way to make Annabel have a little more fun, make her seem more human, a cool thing that they could do that would make for great pictures and video, and something… something that she suddenly wanted to do with the woman who was obviously trying so hard to be… normal.

"Come with me," she said, getting up.

"Where?" asked Annabel.

Indy just gestured at her to follow, beckoning the production twins to come along. This was going to be either disastrous or amazing.

THE SOUNDS of music and singing could be heard from out in the street. Annabel stopped dead outside the door.

"Oh, no."

Indy grinned. "Oh, yes. Come on, trust me for a second, will you?"

"I barely know you."

"Well, this is a chance to get to know me better. You're going to love this, I promise."

"It'll make great publicity," Laura interjected. "This is some good stuff."

Someone inside started an off-key version of a Lady Gaga song and Annabel pulled a face. "I can't do that. I can't sing in front of people."

"Trust me," said Indy. Without thinking, she looped her arm through Annabel's. Annabel needed this. She needed to get out of herself. And Indy loved karaoke, she truly did want to share it with her. "You won't need to sing in front of other people," she added.

Annabel gave her a look, but allowed herself to be led inside.

Music was thumping and a crowd was gathered around the stage, but Indy gave a nod to the barman and led them all through to the back. A line of karaoke boxes waited. Small, private, with glass fronts so you could be seen and not heard.

"Just me and you," Indy said, tugging at Annabel's arm. "Nobody else will hear you. Even Lars and Laura can't fit in there with us." She turned to them. "You'll have to film from outside, sorry."

Annabel sighed, Indy grinned, and she knew she was going to get her way. She danced off to the bar to get the microphones and set up their rental period. As an afterthought, she grabbed two more drinks. Alcohol definitely helped karaoke.

"I can't sing," was the first thing Annabel said when Indy pushed into the box.

"Everyone can sing," Indy said. "You've got a beautiful speaking voice, all you need to do is let yourself do it. And no one will ever hear it except me."

"But—"

"But nothing," Indy said. "You don't care about me. This is all fake, right? So what I think or what I see or hear really doesn't matter at all. You don't need to impress me. Can you honestly say that you're not curious? That you don't want to at least try?"

Annabel's deep blue eyes blinked. Then she shrugged and Indy took that as permission to choose a song. She keyed in what she knew was the perfect number. She handed a microphone to Annabel as the first notes started.

"Come on, I know you know this. Just close your eyes and pretend that you're alone. It's easy."

Indy raised her own microphone for the first line. *"Don't go breaking my heart."*

And to her surprise, Annabel broke in with the next part. *"I couldn't if I tried."*

Her voice was a pleasant alto. She'd been lying, she could sing, though her eyes were still screwed tightly shut. Indy grinned and belted out the next line, letting her musician's soul take over, and as the song progressed she could see Annabel loosening up, could see her body start to move.

Indy shuffled closer, getting ready for the final line, getting closer to Annabel's swaying body, feeling the heat of her, feeling the rhythm in her hips. At the very last moment, she dropped her own microphone, leaning in to duet the last line with Annabel. So close that their cheeks were almost brushing, so close that their lips were almost touching, so close that she could feel electric prickles dancing along her skin.

Her voice failed. Annabel sang the final line alone.

Indy was too busy watching her lips, too busy moving forward to close the distance between them, too busy with the shocking realization that there was nothing that she wanted more in this moment than to kiss Annabel Taylor.

CHAPTER FOURTEEN

At the last second, Annabel turned away. It happened too quickly for Indy to tell whether she'd known what was about to happen or if it had all been in her head.

"That was amazing," Annabel said, not looking in her direction. "I can see why you like it."

"It's fun," Indy said, but her eyes were on Annabel.

Annabel cleared her throat. "You know, uh, that woman in the opposite box, she's been watching you."

Indy looked over and a dark-haired woman raised a glass to her. Automatically, she smiled back.

"You can go and talk to her, if you want," Annabel said awkwardly, still looking through the song list. "Or I could go and talk to her for you, that's the agreement, isn't it?"

"The agreement?" Indy asked.

But she knew exactly what Annabel was talking about and Annabel didn't have a chance to say anything more anyway, because the dark-haired woman was coming over to their box and then she was knocking and then she was pushing the door open and Indy definitely didn't know what she was going to say.

"Hi," the woman said, chirpily. "I don't want to interrupt. I just wanted to see if it was really you. You guys are IndyAnna, right?"

Indy stared at her blankly and Annabel just looked slightly shell-shocked.

"Er, right," the woman said. "I guess you guys are on a date and

I shouldn't... Um, I shouldn't have interrupted. I'm so sorry."

"No, no, it's fine," Indy said, manners kicking in. "Yes, we're IndyAnna. It's nice to meet you."

The woman smiled. "Do you think I could get a picture with you?"

Indy looked over at Annabel who shrugged, but the woman was already beckoning her friend over to take the photo. Indy pulled Annabel into the picture and pasted a big smile over her face. And when they were done, the woman thanked them profusely before running off to show her friends and Indy and Annabel collapsed laughing back into their booth.

"We just got recognized," Indy howled. "How famous are we?"

"Not exactly what I'd imagined being famous for," Annabel said.

"You said it, sister."

For a moment all was still, then Annabel started laughing again and Indy giggled and Annabel pulled up a new song on the list and then they were both singing again.

SUNDAY MORNINGS were relaxing mornings. No alarms, no work, no stress. But Indy was up early anyway. Sun streamed through the windows and she couldn't sleep.

At least she told herself it was because of the sun.

It had absolutely nothing to do with her head being full, not at all.

She was sitting at the kitchen table eating cereal when Lucinda came in.

"Wow, you're an early bird this morning. Or, wait, don't tell me that you haven't been to bed yet?"

"I should be so lucky," Indy said. "No, I'm being an early bird. Too much sun, I can't sleep."

"Have a fun night?" Lucinda asked, opening the fridge.

"Uh, yeah," said Indy, surprised that she actually meant it.

She had had fun with Annabel. Seeing her get down off her high horse, seeing her let go and have fun, she'd seen a totally different side of her. A more approachable, friendlier, and if she was being honest, a more attractive side.

"Do anything fun?"

"Karaoke."

"You're a fountain of conversation this morning," Lucinda said, sitting down with a glass of juice and a yogurt. She squinted at Indy. "What's going on?"

"Nothing!"

"Bullshit. You can't keep things from me, I'm the old wise woman, remember?"

"Who's all of three weeks older than me."

"Wisdom has little to do with chronological age," Lucinda said, licking her spoon. "And you've got a heavy head. The only time you're short of words is when you're too busy thinking about something to articulate it, so what are you thinking about?"

"You know, Annabel and I got recognized last night. Some woman at the karaoke place took a picture with us."

Lucinda nodded. "I didn't want to say anything, but this whole #IndyAnna thing is maybe getting bigger than you think. I keep expecting to see your face on the side of a bus."

"Seriously?"

"It's all over my social media," Lucinda said. "Are you sure this is what you signed up for?"

"Free publicity is no bad thing, surely? It gets my name and my face out there." Which was true.

"So that's not what's bothering you," Lucinda said, squinting at her again. "So what is it that's running around that little mind of yours? Is this Annabel turning out to be an even bigger bitch than you expected."

"No!" The word came out hard and fast and Lucinda raised an eyebrow high enough that Indy knew she suspected something. She sighed. "We almost kissed last night."

Lucinda took another mouthful of yogurt. "You both almost kissed? Or you almost kissed her? Or she almost kissed you?"

"Er, I don't know. I thought I saw something there, but then maybe it was just me. Maybe I almost kissed her."

"And would that be a bad thing?"

"I'm not supposed to be dating, remember?"

"Not what I'm talking about," Lucinda said. "What do you think would happen if you kissed her?"

"She'd probably slap me," Indy said.

Lucinda put her yogurt pot down. "Do you want to kiss her? I mean now, in the bright light of day, without a drink inside you?"

"Of course not!"

Lucinda just looked at her for a long minute, then picked her yogurt up again. "Okay, whatever you say."

She didn't, did she? Okay, maybe Annabel wasn't quite the cold, stand-offish person she'd first imagined, maybe she was physically attractive, maybe she could let loose and have a little fun when she wasn't being shy or under-confident or whatever the hell was going on. But that didn't mean she wanted to actually, really kiss her.

On the other hand, did it mean that she actually, really *didn't* want to kiss her?

It had been a while, almost two weeks, since she'd been on a real date, since she'd had intimate contact with anyone. And it had been a long while, far too long, since she'd been fully intimate with anyone. Maybe it was all just catching up with her. Maybe this was just withdrawal after stopping dating cold turkey.

She was rescued from having to think about Annabel even more, or, worse, having to discuss the matter further with Lucinda, by her phone ringing in her bedroom.

She didn't know anyone who would call her on a Sunday morning. Except perhaps Annabel. She put on a spurt of speed and made it to her room just in time to pick up the phone.

"Hey."

"Hello, is that Indigo?"

Her heartbeat slowed down a little. Not much, but a little. It wasn't Annabel. But she was still excited. "Yes."

"This is Dan Rivers. Sorry to call you on a Sunday, but we do seem to keep missing each other."

"Oh, it's no problem, no problem at all," she said, trying to stop her voice squeaking in excitement. She sat down on the edge of her bed, slightly afraid that her legs were shaking so much from excitement that they might not hold her up for much longer.

"Well, it's nice to finally talk to you." There was a touch of humor in his voice. "Now, I'll get straight to business, I don't want to take up any more of your Sunday than necessary. I really would like to talk to you about representation. I'm assuming you don't currently have an agent?"

"No, no I don't." She had to slam her mouth shut to stop more words pouring out she was so excited.

"Great. But I'd also really like to hear you play again before we get to real specifics. Do you have any gigs coming up?"

She thought quickly. "Uh, yes, I'll be at the same coffee shop next Thursday. And I'll be playing at an indy music festival on the West Side the Saturday after that."

There was a pause. "Hmm. Neither of those work for me, unfortunately."

Her heart dropped a little. But then he spoke again.

"It's a little unorthodox, but why don't you bring your guitar over to my place one night this week? I don't normally do this, but, well, I think you're something special and I really do need to hear you play again."

And that thudding heartbeat was back again. She grinned so wide that her face hurt. "Absolutely, not a problem at all. And thank you for making an exception for me, I really appreciate you going out of your way."

He chuckled. "Not a problem. I'll text you the address. Does Tuesday work for you?"

"Yes, any time, whatever you need."

Another chuckle. "Great, I'll look forward to it. Bye, Indigo."

She danced around the apartment, clutching the phone to her chest. This could be the big time. This could really be it. She didn't spare another thought for Annabel for the rest of the morning.

CHAPTER FIFTEEN

Annabel's feet pounded on the sidewalk as she left her building. It was barely light, but early morning was the only time she could fit a run in. Besides, she liked the quiet, liked the city before it woke up properly. Even on a Sunday.

As she ran, her breath came in short spurts and her leg muscles burned. In a good way. A way that could almost let her forget about the night before.

She was no idiot. She might not have ever fallen in love but even she hadn't been able to miss it. A moment. A... thing. A shiver, a look, a glance, a stillness. Indy had leaned into that microphone and then, suddenly, she had been close. And then, suddenly, Annabel had seen her properly.

It was a little like waking up in a strange room. There was instant unfamiliarity followed by something altogether different, a comforting realization that yes, you knew where you were, yes this was perfectly good and fine.

All this time she'd closed her eyes to Indy, assumed that she was as hippy as her name, that she was a bad match, a flaw in the algorithm. But here was the thing: what if she wasn't?

She rounded a corner and jogged down to the river path, letting the cold morning air burn on her face as she ran.

What if Indy was a match after all? Was that a crazy thought? Was that just the wishful thinking of a lonely woman who had never let anyone into her life?

The evening had built up to it, she could see that now. The beginning had been awkward, but then Indy had played along and the conversation that had been so stilted had become smoother and more interesting. And then Indy had started to talk about music and a light had come on inside her and a passion glowed through her skin.

It was like she'd come alive all of a sudden, and she radiated a warmth that Annabel had longed to get closer to. But still she hadn't realized.

She hadn't realized until that moment, when Indy was leaning in, when the microphone was solid in her hand, when those lips were so close to her. Only then had it hit her. Hit her like a brick to the head.

Indy was attractive.

No, that wasn't quite right.

She was attracted to Indy.

She ran harder, hopping up the embankment and then down again to avoid a woman with a yapping dog.

Seeing Indy come alive that way, hearing her sing, letting herself take part in the evening instead of sitting at the side or leaving early, it had all affected her more than she thought.

But she'd broken the moment, she'd turned away and she was glad now that she had. Yes, her heart was a little lighter. Perhaps the algorithm wasn't as broken as she'd thought, perhaps her initial effort had been good enough. Yes, she found Indy attractive. But that wasn't the first time this had happened and it wouldn't be the last.

Finding someone attractive was not at all the same thing as acting on that attraction. She had ignored these spiky feelings of desire before and knew that she'd have no problem ignoring them again. She had to wait it out, wait until their deal was done and Indy was gone and then she could let out a sigh and carry on.

Would it be such a bad thing?

The voice in her head nagged at her.

Yes, yes it would. This was business and you didn't mix business with pleasure. This was an unsuitable match, even though perhaps it wasn't as unsuitable as she'd initially thought. This was nothing more than a momentary feeling of lust, a stabbing that she could ignore and work through. No different from all the other times.

Her way was cleaner, easier, more logical.

The other way would be... messier, sweatier, sliding and slipping and touching and tasting until she didn't know where she ended and Indy began and...

Her breath hitched and she tripped, stretching out her arms to stop her going headlong into the river. She landed with a bump on one knee and slowly lowered the rest of her body to the ground as pain blossomed through her.

"Fuck."

There was no one there to hear it. Her knee throbbed.

"Fuck!" she shouted again.

Lusting after a woman because she'd sung a song, wanting someone because they showed passion, getting lonely and desperate and making bad decisions.

"Fuck!" she yelled at the top of her lungs into the early morning fog.

HER KNEE felt slightly better on Monday morning, but she still limped into the office. She detoured past Billy's door, but it was closed. Closed and almost nine o'clock. She knocked, but there was no answer and she hadn't expected one. Billy wasn't here.

What the hell was going on with him?

She was reluctant to press him, but she was also starting to get worried.

"No sign of Billy?" she asked as she passed Laura in the corridor.

"Nope," Laura said. "But I'm glad you're here. The pictures of you and Indy at karaoke are trending through the roof. It'd be great if we could do a quick follow up. Maybe coffee or dinner or something? Something calm to contrast with the karaoke action."

Annabel took a breath. She didn't feel ready to face Indy yet. But it was better to get back on the horse. She was pretty certain that Indy had no idea that she'd been thinking about kissing her, so there was little reason to be shy about it.

"I'll see what I can set up," she said.

But back in her office she found herself procrastinating, not wanting to place the call, doodling on a pad next to the phone.

Which was when she remembered the other important thing that had happened on Saturday night. The bucket list.

The idea had sounded stupid and brilliant at the same time. Such a simple way of making goals, but maybe it was something that she needed. Rather than walking around hoping to bump into hobbies that she wanted, maybe what she really needed was a bucket list, something to encourage her to get out there and do things.

It was a stupid idea.

But maybe it could work for her. Maybe she just needed more... instruction in her life. Because she did want to make changes, she knew she couldn't rely on Billy forever, knew that she wouldn't be working with LBN forever.

She opened up a file on her computer and lined it with check-boxes and then thought for a second.

Okay, the first one was easy.

Get a job in silicon valley.

She thought for a second more, then added:

Sing karaoke.

With a grin, she ticked off that box. What came next? What did she really want to do?

Go to Paris.

There was something everyone wanted to do. This was easier than she thought. Building a list of interests outside of work wasn't impossible. She bit her lip. What next? She had to be honest if she was doing this. Really honest.

Make a friend that isn't Billy. Or Cassie.

She felt heavier at the idea of it, at the fact that she needed to even write it down, and she rushed into the next entry without thought.

Fall in love.

The words glared back up at her, cursor ticking next to them. She stared at them. Jesus, what was wrong with her?

She closed down the file without saving it, deleting the entire list. She had work to do and she needed to do it, screwing around with some stupid, infantile bucket list wasn't going to make her big bucks.

And part of her job was being professional and keeping to the agreement she'd made with Billy. The karaoke pictures were trending, and that was great, but it meant a fast follow up. No time to procrastinate. Take advantage of the opportunities they'd been given.

She was dialing the number before she could give things much more thought.

"Indy."

"It's me."

"Oh. Hey there, my little chanteuse."

"Chanteuse?"

"It means singer, it's..." Annabel heard the sigh down the phone. "Nothing. Never mind. What is it?"

"We're trending and need a quick follow up on that karaoke date," Annabel said briskly. "Nothing big. A coffee date maybe and as soon as possible. Can you do tomorrow?"

There was a slight pause. "Sure, if it's important."

"It's important."

"Okay, well, I've got an audition with an agent. I'm not sure how long that'll last, but I can do a quick coffee after?"

"That works." It would give her more time in the office, anyway. "Where's the audition at?"

"Um, it's at the guy's apartment, somewhere just off Fifth Street?"

Annabel was about to agree when she stopped, thought, then asked incredulously: "You're meeting this guy at his apartment?"

Indy laughed. "It's fine. It just happened to work out that way since we're both so busy. You don't need to act the maiden aunt. I'll be fine."

Annabel blew out a breath. She didn't have a great feeling about this, but it was Indy's business, not hers. "Okay, right. I'll find a coffee place close to there and text you where we are. I'll be there at around eight? I can wait around if necessary." The place would have wi-fi, she could always work.

"Perfect," Indy said.

And Annabel hung up, still a little queasy. Though whether from talking to Indy herself and hearing that voice again, or from the idea that Indy was fine going to a strange guy's apartment, she couldn't really tell.

CHAPTER SIXTEEN

She shouldn't have gone. She knew that now. Knew that the stories, the warnings, the stereotypes, they were all there for a reason. She shouldn't have gone but she had and now she felt shaky and sick inside.

Shaky and sick as she wandered the streets, circling the block again and again. Shaky and sick as she finally walked into the coffee shop. Shaky and sick as she saw Annabel's face.

And then Annabel was holding her, kissing her cheek and she could feel Lars and Laura darting around, taking pictures and she didn't have the strength to stop them.

It was Annabel that did. "Stop."

Lars and Laura stopped fluttering. Annabel lifted Indy's chin with her finger and looked at her. Then she turned back to Lars and Laura. "That's enough for tonight."

"But—" Laura moved closer to protest and then saw Indy's face and she nodded. "Yeah, okay, sure."

"No," Indy said. She'd already screwed everything up. She couldn't screw this up as well. "No, it's fine. Let's get coffee."

Laura blinked, glanced over at Lars, and shook her head. "No, we're cool. We got shots of you coming in, shots of that awesome hello hug. That's enough. We can do something with that. Make it all mysterious. Don't worry, we're good here."

She was already packing stuff away, Lars too. And Indy felt Annabel take her arm and steer her out of the coffee shop, away from all the eyes.

"What's wrong?"

"Nothing," Indy said automatically.

"Bullshit," said Annabel. "I know I'm not always great at relating to people, but I'm not actually stupid. You're white as a sheet and you're trembling and you look like you're about to faint or puke or both."

Indy said nothing as people pushed by them on the sidewalk. Then Annabel sighed and hailed a cab and bundled her inside, giving an address to the driver before she climbed in too.

ANNABEL'S APARTMENT was exactly what she would have expected if she'd had time to think about being allowed inside. Minimalist, with clean lines and sharp edges. A lot like Annabel herself, truth be told. It was warm though, and quiet, and peaceful in its own way.

Indy propped her guitar case up by the door, kicked her shoes off and Annabel was chattering about something, alcohol maybe, or perhaps the weather, but she wasn't listening. She was busy feeling safe, feeling calmer for the first time that evening. And when Annabel took her to a large couch she let herself fall into it and a glass was pushed into her hand. Whiskey. Warm and potent.

"What happened?" Annabel perched beside her.

"Is it really that obvious? Do I look that bad?"

Annabel considered her, eyes navy blue and narrowed. She nodded. "You look pretty bad," she confessed.

Indy sighed. There were worse stories, she knew. She'd heard plenty worse from other women. More than that, she was embarrassed. And embarrassed about the fact that she was embarrassed. And then she started to feel shaky and sick again.

"You went to this agent's apartment," Annabel said softly.

Indy closed her eyes and nodded, seeing the ornate elevator, seeing the large front door, hearing the doorbell as she rang it, hope beating in her heart.

"Then what happened?" Annabel asked, still softly, still gently, as though she was talking to a small child.

Indy took a deep breath. "It wasn't what it was supposed to be."

"He wasn't what he was supposed to be, you mean," said Annabel and it wasn't a question.

Anger spiked in Indy's chest and overcame her embarrassment for a second. "He opened the door in his bath robe and I should have known then."

Maybe she had. But she hadn't acted on it. She'd been too busy thinking about the opportunity, thinking that something like this wouldn't, couldn't happen to someone like her. Too busy being polite and not wanting to offend the man because he obviously meant no harm. He was rich and powerful and why would he be interested in someone like her?

"What happened then?" prompted Annabel.

Indy licked her dry lips, sipped at the whiskey. "I went inside. I put my guitar case down, just like I did here. I tried to shake his hand, but he went in for a kiss instead. He…"

He got closer and she bent her head so he could graze her cheek with an air kiss except once that had happened he didn't back off. He turned her head toward him instead and made to kiss her lips and she tried to take a step backward but found she was against the wall and he was coming closer and closer…

"He tried to kiss me," she managed to say.

Annabel's hand tightened around hers and she hadn't realized that her hand was being held. "I'll kill him."

She wasn't sure that she'd heard the words right until she saw the murderous look on Annabel's face. "He didn't do anything, he didn't, really," she said, embarrassment flaring again. She was making a fuss over nothing. "I slipped by him, grabbed my stuff and walked right out. Nothing else happened."

"He took advantage of you, that's more than enough."

"I should have known better, you tried to warn me, I'm not an idiot, I know what can happen. I should have known better than to go to his apartment."

That murderous look flashed again over Annabel's face. "No, don't say that. Don't ever say that. You're not to blame for some idiot man's uncontrollable urges. He's the asshole here. You're not responsible."

She lightened a little just hearing the words. "It sucked," she said, drinking more whisky and starting to feel more herself. "It sucked but it could have been worse. Much worse. I was lucky."

"That's one way of putting it," Annabel said. She stopped, swallowed, then looked at Indy. "We should go to the police."

Indy shook her head. "What's the point? He didn't do anything in the end, it'll be his word against mine, and I can't. I can't have people feeling sorry for me like that, I can't go over it again and again just for nothing to happen to him."

"And when he does this to someone else?"

She felt a rush of heat. "I can't be responsible for other people right now," she said, knowing it was selfish but also true.

Annabel squeezed her hand tighter. "Okay."

"Maybe later, maybe tomorrow." She stared into her glass knowing that it wouldn't be tomorrow or anytime soon. She wanted to forget about all of this, forget it had happened, forget that she'd been so thoughtless, so stupid.

"What?" Annabel asked.

Indy snorted, a small sign of returning normality. "For someone that's generally crap at being around other people you're extraordinarily observant tonight."

Annabel rolled her eyes. "Just tell me. Whatever it is that's on your mind. We're already here, we're already talking, you might as well get it all out."

"It's just that this is so me."

"This isn't your fault," Annabel said again.

"That's not what I meant. I meant that I always have this hope. I went there tonight thinking that this could be my big chance. This could really be it for me. And it turned into shit. Just like when I met—" She brought herself up short.

"Just like when you met me," supplied Annabel. Her hand was getting warmer. "Just like when you thought you'd be meeting your soulmate and you got me instead."

Annabel's hand was soft, softer than Indy had imagined. Her eyes were sad and large and her warmth was palpable. She could smell the light scent of her, smell coconut from her shampoo, could see the way her hair looped over her ear, could see a small series of lines beginning to collect at the corner of her eye.

And she wanted to pull in, to get closer, to…

No.

No. This was Annabel. This was Annabel who was rude and abrupt, who had zero interests outside of work, who was cold and terrible around other people. This was Annabel that was so laden with flaws that she was just a whole big knot of things that Indy absolutely and definitely wasn't interested in.

This wasn't her soulmate. No matter what some stupid algorithm promised.

This wasn't someone that she wanted to pull into a gentle kiss that got heated until they were tearing at each other's clothes.

But Annabel was here. Annabel was holding her hand, she was angry on her behalf, she'd comforted her and listened to her and was protective of her. And Annabel was beautiful and sexy in a stiff-suited way. And…

Indy cleared her throat. "I think that I'd like to go home now."

Annabel raised an eyebrow. "Is there someone there? I don't like the idea of you going home alone."

"It was a shock," Indy said, trying to keep the tremor out of her voice because that wasn't the only shock she'd had this evening. It was just as shocking, more shocking even, to discover that her traitorous heart was starting to like Annabel. Really like her.

"Indy."

Those lips saying her name. "It was just a shock," she said again. "A nasty one, but I was lucky, I escaped unscathed. I'll be okay, Annabel. I can handle this." She paused and Annabel looked doubtful and somehow it made it all worse that she was being considerate. "Lucinda will be there, my room-mate."

And finally, Annabel nodded. "I'll get you a cab," she said.

CHAPTER SEVENTEEN

The problem was that it hadn't been a problem. She'd brought Indy back to her apartment like it was nothing, without a second thought. Her heart had about broken when she'd seen the look on Indy's face as she walked into the coffee shop, and she'd guessed immediately the nature of what had happened.

She'd opened her arms and taken her in and she'd sheltered her the best she knew how and taken her home. All without considering the fact that this was *not the sort of thing she did*. Ever.

Yes, there had been lovers, but in hotels, never in her apartment. But with Indy it had seemed... natural.

Seeing her sitting there on the couch hadn't made her feel sick or disturbed or wary or scared. It hadn't made her feel anything other than... at home. Which she should have felt anyway because it was her damn apartment but Indy had somehow made it feel more home.

And she'd wanted to kick that agent right in the crotch. She'd wanted to humiliate him and punish him and yet she'd still sat back when Indy had said she didn't want to go to the police. It was her right. She'd sat back and listened and then her heart had just about broken all over again when Indy had thought it had been her shot, when Indy had done all but confess to the fact that she'd thought she'd be meeting her soulmate.

Annabel was a disappointment.

It stung to think about.

Stung so much that when she rounded the corner and saw that Billy's office was once again empty she kicked out at the door.

Damn Billy.

Damn Indy.

Damn herself for being so… not herself.

She pulled out her phone and was half-way through a nasty message to Billy when she pushed open her office door and saw Billy lounging in her desk chair.

Time to put Indy away. And time to put an end to all this. They'd played with feelings long enough. She couldn't be a disappointment anymore, she needed to let Indy go.

"Where have you been?" she snarled.

Billy raised an eyebrow. "Um, right here, waiting for you in your empty office, which leads me to think that the real question is where have you been?"

She paused for a moment. Was it that late? No, Billy was screwing with her. And she really wasn't in the mood. She wasn't in the mood to be here, to be in her office, to work, to talk to Billy, to do any of the things that she normally did, that she normally wanted to do.

What was she in the mood for?

Whisky. Something she never drank. Whisky on the couch in her own warm apartment. With Indy at the other end, cradling her glass, a mere arm's length away, within touching distance, looking like she belonged there, looking like the apartment had been built around her.

It was like she'd tasted something unexpectedly glorious and couldn't wait to take another mouthful.

Tasted something poisonous, she reminded herself. Something that she mustn't taste again. Out of fairness to herself and to Indy. This needed to stop.

"You're never here," she snapped at Billy, provoking him to

give herself time to think about how she was going to go about breaking their deal.

"Not true."

He looked so wounded that she calmed a little and sat down at least. "It is true. You're not here half the time. What's going on?"

He grinned and ruffled his hair and shook his head. "Nothing, not a thing."

It hurt that he wouldn't tell her, that he'd lie to her so obviously. Billy was supposed to be her friend. "Listen," she started. She was just going to tell him, just going to spit it out and if he got angry then so be it.

"Hold on," said Billy. "There's something we need to talk about first."

He looked weary so maybe he was going to tell her. Maybe he wasn't going to keep secrets from her. So she closed her mouth, willing to listen.

"I got a call yesterday from a production company."

Annabel blinked, confused. "Okay."

"The thing is," he said, leaning forward over her desk. "The thing is, they want to make a web series. Just something short. They'd use video we already have for the first episode or two. But obviously they'd like to film some more. Laura and Lars are both on board with it, so you won't be dealing with a bunch of strangers. There'd be some production staff around, but..."

It took her that long to catch up with what he was saying and to process it into anything that came even close to making sense.

"Hold on. What?"

Billy sighed and she knew that he'd been trying to sneak the idea past her, explaining it before she cottoned on. "A web series."

"About me and Indy."

He nodded. "That's about the deal. It'll be a spur of the moment thing, obviously, unscripted, short little episodes. But I gotta say, it looks like a good deal for us. They'll reap the advertising profits and we'll get the sign-ups."

"A web series about me and Indy," she said again.

"Yes. #IndyAnna is a big thing, Annabel. It's really taking off. I'm not sure that you really understand just how much, you're hardly a social media maven. And I know. I know it's not what you agreed to, I know—"

"I'm not sure what you know anymore, Billy. I'm not sure what's happening around here anymore. I don't want to do this and I'm sure you know that I don't. In fact, I want out of this whole thing. It's ridiculous. It was a marketing ploy and it worked in the short-term, but we can't keep pretending like this."

Billy said nothing. He reached into his pocket, pulled out a piece of paper and slid it across the desk, her desk, to her. Annabel picked it up, read it and frowned.

"What's this?"

"I didn't say anything because I didn't want to get your hopes up," he said. "But I met with a potential buyer on Monday. That's what was offered for LBN."

She looked down again at the number with its impossible amount of zeroes. She felt a shudder go down her back. Money like this was life-changing. More than life-changing. Money like this was what they'd been working for, what the lack of social life, lack of hobbies, lack of anything but work had all been about. Money like this would let them both do anything they pleased for the rest of their lives. She felt like she'd been punched in the stomach.

"And if that's the valuation right now," Billy said. "Imagine what it'll be a month from now after a successful web series and all the free advertising and sign-ups that come with it. With a happy ever after love story to prove that our algorithm really works."

Except it really didn't work. Did it? Annabel couldn't take her eyes off the paper. Was this what Billy had been hiding from her? Instinctively, she knew it wasn't the whole story, knew that there was more, but she was too busy thinking to dig further. She had enough on her plate right now without trying to solve Billy's mysteries.

"Can you persuade Indy?" Billy asked.

Not 'can you persuade yourself' because Billy had already decided that she'd do it. He was right. She'd sacrificed so much to get where she was that another month was nothing. She didn't want to be part of some stupid web series, but she'd do it. She'd do it to get the whole rest of her life to do as she pleased.

And Indy? Indy sitting on her couch and sipping whisky and smelling like fabric softener and cotton? Indy would have to do this with her. She wasn't about to give her a choice.

Indy could profit from this. She could. She really could have her shot. And if Annabel had to make that decision for her, then she would. Because getting your face out there, getting your talent recognized, that was how you got your shot. Not through meeting some sleazy agent in his bathrobe.

She ignored the rest. Ignored that she was actually starting to like Indy, ignored that maybe she was being selfish, definitely ignored that she wanted to hold Indy in her arms again. She ignored what was probably nothing more than an emotional hiccup. Because her whole life had been leading up to the moment that she signed a deal to sell her first company.

And the moment was so tantalizingly close that she could smell it.

So could she persuade Indy to go along with it?

"I'll persuade her," she said with full confidence.

Billy grinned and leaped up and kissed her cheeks and hollered in excitement and started dancing around her office yelling that they were going to be rich.

Annabel smiled. But in her head she was thinking about how she was going to explain this to Indy. How she was going to spend another month, a month under scrutiny by camera and the public and who knew who else, with a woman that she could never be attracted to. A woman that she was undeniably attracted to, though thinking about it made her feel tremulous inside.

She'd give Indy whatever it was she asked for. Anything. No limits. And Indy would say yes. She was sure of it.

CHAPTER EIGHTEEN

"No."

It was a gut reaction, but that didn't mean it was a bad one. A web series? Not a chance.

"Why not?" Annabel asked, quite reasonably.

She was sitting on the couch in her apartment and Indy was sinking into the cushions beside her. It was strange. Her second time here and already she knew the smell of it, felt like she'd been here a million times before.

Why not? She needed an answer. An answer that wasn't the truth, because the truth was that she was terrified. Terrified that being on film would mean that someone would spot what she was beginning to be sure of: that she actually liked Annabel. More than liked. With all her flaws and her coldness and everything else. She liked her.

The heart wants what the heart wants, she'd tried to tell herself. Which didn't go a whole long way to explaining why she was suddenly crushing hard on someone who really shouldn't be for her.

"Because I don't want to," she said truculently.

Annabel sighed. "That's a stupid answer."

Indy shook her head. See, one minute she was thinking about how she liked the woman, and the next she was thinking about slapping her. That was just how screwed up this all was. "Why are you like this?" she asked suddenly, the question springing out so fast it took even her by surprise.

"Like what?" asked Annabel.

"This," Indy said, the question was already asked, she might as well get an answer. "Cold and terrible around people? It's not that you can't treat people well, can't be considerate. I've seen you, experienced you, being absolutely lovely." Like just the other night, something she really didn't want to think about right now. "So why do you act most of the time like you hate all people? Like their feelings don't matter and you don't give a damn about anyone but yourself?"

Annabel's mouth opened and then slammed shut again and Indy knew she'd touched a nerve. But was Annabel going to give her a solid answer? She had a feeling that the question needed an answer, for both their sakes. She shouldn't have asked it, it was rude, but it was important.

"You really want to know?"

She wasn't sure if the look on Annabel's face was defeat or horror or disgust or just plain anger at her rudeness in asking. But she nodded anyway. Because she really did want to know. She was curious about what made Annabel tick.

"I was the nerd. The dork. The geek. Whatever you like to call it," Annabel said.

She wasn't looking at Indy. She was staring far off into the distance into a place that she'd tried to block out, tried to run away from.

"I had glasses, I wore t-shirts from Wal-Mart, I was interested in math and science and nothing else. I was..." She took a breath. "I was not perfect."

A little piece of her ice melted away and Indy saw vulnerability for the first time. She wanted to speak, but forced herself to keep quiet. Let Annabel tell this her way.

Annabel straightened her shoulders. "I was bullied. Permanently. From kindergarten all the way up to graduation. Every school day. My books were taken, my clothes were ripped, I was humiliated and scorned and made to feel like I took up space in a world where I didn't belong. Do you have any idea how that felt?

How it still feels?"

Indy didn't move.

"No, of course you don't," Annabel said. "How could you? You're beautiful and perfect and play music and make friends. But I wasn't like that. God, how I wished I was. But I couldn't change myself into you. Couldn't become popular. So I did the only other thing that I could do."

And Indy found her voice. "You stopped caring."

"I pretended to stop caring," Annabel said. "Yes. It was the only way to survive. To pretend that I didn't care because I hated everyone anyway. I made it all alone. I did all this myself. I've proven myself over and over, I've shown that I don't need anyone else."

There was a long pause and Indy felt Annabel trying to gather herself, to control what she could, not to let emotions out. And the thought of that, the thought of containing all that hatred for so many years, the thought of Annabel thinking of herself as anything less than beautiful and wonderful, was enough to make her do it.

She didn't remember moving. Didn't remember anything until she was right there, until she was cupping Annabel's chin in her hand and looking into those deep blue eyes and not even thinking about what she was doing because the thought of it was enough to scare the living hell out of her.

Their lips met. Softly at first. Tentatively. She leaned in, tasted the mint of toothpaste and the bitterness of coffee. Smelled Annabel, the rose and musk scent of her. She felt her heartbeat speed up and her blood begin rushing through her veins and then she was leaning in even closer and Annabel was kissing her back and she was floating up and free and pressing herself into Annabel with a desire she'd never felt before.

It was Annabel that pulled away.

❊ ❊ ❊

"What was that?"

Annabel calmed her breathing, tried to process what had just happened. But it was impossible. She just knew that for a second there she'd forgotten herself. Forgotten her promises to herself, forgotten her past, forgotten everything except Indy. It was terrifying. And wonderful.

"I like you," Indy said. She backed off a little, giving Annabel space.

"You like me?"

Indy bit her lip. "Look, I know. We're not right for each other. We both said so. And you're right, you're not perfect. But then, I guess, neither am I. And the longer we're together, the more time we spend together, the more I think that maybe we were wrong. Maybe we're not so bad together. I usually walk out at the first sign of a flaw, but with you I didn't have that option but the attraction is still there."

"Attraction?"

She was still breathing hard. Attraction. Indy was attracted to her. She was attracted to Indy. There was no argument in her brain from that. She'd known. Known since she'd seen Indy sitting on her couch. Known that maybe being alone wasn't the only option, that having someone wasn't necessarily as bad as she'd imagined.

"Attraction," Indy said firmly. "I am attracted to you. I like you. You grew on me, what can I say? I liked that you were angry for me the other day, I liked that you didn't push me into doing anything, I like that you just listened to me. I like that you're passionate about your work and that you know what you want and you're ambitious. I like the way you look, the way you smell, the way you taste. I could go on."

She looked exhausted and Annabel found herself laughing. "You like me."

"Yes. And you don't want to be with anyone, I know that, but we have to be together anyway so I don't really see the harm in this."

"The harm in what?" Even though she knew the answer, she

wanted to hear Indy say it, wanted to know that this wasn't a trick.

Indy sighed. "Look, if we're going to do this web series thing we have to spend a little more time together. So why don't we? A relationship can develop, you know, it doesn't have to be love at first sight. We have time to prove ourselves. I can prove to you that being with someone isn't as disastrous as you might think. That maybe it's pretty nice."

"And I can prove to you what?" Annabel said, only half kidding. "That you can love me despite my flaws?"

"That I can love anyone despite their flaws. That your flaws are what make you you and that without them you wouldn't be you and I wouldn't be interested."

Indy's hair was pulled back revealing the freckles on her cheekbones and just how turquoise her eyes really were. Annabel longed to put her hands on Indy's waist, to pull her in, to discover just what was under that long skirt. But something was stopping her.

"I'm not a disappointment to you?"

Indy frowned. "A disappointment?"

"When you first met me, you thought you were going to meet your soulmate and then you met me instead and I was a disappointment."

Indy bit her lip. "I'm not going to lie."

"Good, because I have a hard enough time trusting people as it is."

"Yes, you were a disappointment. Not because you weren't attractive, you are, very. But because you weren't what I was looking for. But then, maybe I was just looking for the wrong thing. Is that so hard to believe?"

"No, I suppose."

"Then why can't we try this?"

Annabel rubbed her face. "There's a lot of money in this for me," she said, wanting to stay honest. "This web series should make the price of LBN skyrocket and then both Billy and I intend to sell. I am doing this for money, not just for you."

"I understand that," Indy said. "And I'm not exactly doing it out of the goodness of my heart either. Getting my face out there, becoming recognizable will be good for my career too. But that doesn't mean we can't also use this as a trial to see if perhaps we're better suited than we think."

Annabel stopped. "Is this on your bucket list? Being on TV?"

"Nope," Indy said. "Not at all. Falling in love is on my bucket list."

She could get hurt. She'd opened her heart to Indy without meaning to. She'd had no intention of mentioning her past, the bullying, the misery that she thought she'd left behind. But she'd done it anyway and here was Indy, admitting that maybe she'd made a mistake and maybe they could have something.

And Annabel wanted that.

More than she'd ever realized.

She wanted someone. No, not someone. Indy. She wanted Indy.

It was a risk, but so was everything. A risk that maybe she was more ready for than she thought.

"Okay. We do it," she said decisively. "We do the series and we do this, us, whatever this is. We try it."

She wanted to say more but Indy was already moving, was twisting herself, straddling her and pushing her back into the couch and then kissing her so long and hard that Annabel could barely breathe.

And she let herself disappear into it, not caring for the moment about anything other than the feeling of Indy's lips on hers.

CHAPTER NINETEEN

They were sitting in a bar, soft drinks on the table, and Indy couldn't help but feel like she was being interviewed. Which was weird, since the company wanted her, not the other way around.

"From your point of view, nothing should really change," Barbara was saying.

Barbara was their director, a tall woman dressed in cargo pants with too many pockets, glasses on top of her head, tangled in her greying hair. She looked determined and gruff and more than a little scary.

Indy reached out and took Annabel's hand. It still felt new, being able to touch her in this way. She noticed Laura noticing the action and smiled to herself. She'd wondered how long it would take Lars and Laura to figure out that they weren't faking it anymore.

"Nothing should change," Annabel echoed.

"No," said Barbara. "I mean, I'll be around a little more, just to ensure that we're getting the kind of shots I want. But mostly you'll just do what you did before, go out, have fun, and completely ignore Lars and Laura who'll still be shooting. That's it."

"Okay," Indy said, looking at Annabel. "I guess we can do that."

"Why mess with a good thing?" Barbara asked with a toothy grin. "You guys are trending left, right, and center, and all we want to do is capitalize on that. Which should be easy enough.

So, no big demands from me."

"That's a relief," Indy said, knowing she was speaking for Annabel too. They'd been unsure of what would be expected of them.

"We do need to think about a big ending," Barbara said, flipping open her old-school phone and checking it. "A proposal, a declaration of love, something to that effect. Something to really go out with a bang. But we have time to discuss that. We'll need a nice way to wrap things up."

She looked up at Lars and Laura who were sitting in silence, either over-awed at the thought of working with a real director or, more likely, irritated that they had to put their phones down for more than a minute.

"You two ready?" she asked.

They nodded in sync.

"Then we'll be off," said Barbara. "Give us ten minutes or so to get set up, and then you two can come in whenever you like and start having your date. It'd be great if you could come in separately."

And then they were gone, disappearing off to the bowling alley across the street where Indy and Annabel were to have their next filmed date.

"See, not so bad, right?" Indy asked.

Annabel was still holding her hand, fingers tickling gently at her palm and Indy felt a stab of wanting go through her.

"Not so bad," Annabel agreed. "Although now that we're here I'm not so sure that it's wise for us to be filmed."

"This is all your idea," Indy protested. But she'd seen the glint in Annabel's eye, she knew exactly what was going on.

"Yes, you're correct. But now I have to keep my hands off you or risk turning this entire show into an X-rated series, which definitely isn't what Barbara or Billy had in mind."

As she talked, she was coming closer, close enough that her lips brushed against Indy's ear and another stabbing of lust went through her.

This was... different. Exciting even. It was like a dam had

broken and suddenly they'd discovered something about themselves and Indy wanted nothing more than complete privacy to uncover all of Annabel's secrets.

Which she wasn't going to get.

She sighed, knowing it had been far too long since the last time she'd slept with anyone, and also knowing that it was too soon to be thinking about sleeping with Annabel. This situation was so new, so fragile, that she didn't want to risk ruining it. Not just yet.

"Do you know how famous we are?" she asked, pulling back a little.

Annabel shrugged. A tendril of her dark red hair had come loose and she tucked it behind her ear. "Honestly, I don't really do social media."

"Me neither," Indy said, pulling out her phone. "But I've got accounts. And I kind of feel like we should probably know what people are saying about us, no?"

As she spoke, she was typing, anything to keep her mind off Annabel's hand sliding slowly up her leg. And then she felt cold and a little sick. She turned her phone to face Annabel.

"Jesus."

"Jesus indeed."

Millions of results. Videos, pictures, web pages, tags, everything that it took to be anyone online. For the first time she saw her own face staring out at her from a list of search results and it left her feeling a little shaky.

"You did want a little recognition," Annabel said.

Indy nodded but quickly switched her phone off. "This might be more than I'd bargained for," she said. She looked up at Annabel. "It's kind of scary."

"Which is exactly why I haven't been prowling around the internet searching for us," said Annabel. "And we need to get a move on. Shall I go first?"

Indy nodded and let Annabel slide out of their booth. She missed the warmth of Annabel's body next to hers.

THERE WAS the clatter of pins falling as she walked in. Annabel was standing by one of the lanes and they casually brushed cheeks in greeting. It hadn't been discussed but Indy was glad of it. Glad that Annabel somehow knew not to kiss her right then in front of the cameras.

They got set up with shoes and drinks and she even persuaded Annabel to partake in a pitcher of beer, which made her screw her nose up in distaste but she drank it anyway and Indy smiled. And then it was down to the business of the date itself.

The view wasn't bad, she thought, as she sat back, watching Annabel bowl in tight jeans, the roundness of her backside, the curve of her waist making her mouth water.

Not bad, but there was nothing she could do about it right this minute. So she needed to concentrate on bowling.

She took her turn, choosing a ball that was too heavy so it disappeared into the gutter half way down the lane.

"No," Annabel said. "Here, use this ball instead." She picked up a red one and handed it over, their hands brushing.

"Thanks."

But Annabel didn't sit down. "You need to bend here," she said, tapping at Indy's knee. "And then here," she added, tapping at Indy's thigh. "And, of course, here," her hand slid into the curve of her waist and Indy's mouth went dry with want.

"Right," she squeaked, taking a step back.

Annabel grinned and Indy swore under her breath. She hadn't taken Annabel for cruel, for a game-player, for anything other than a straight-shooter. But she'd been wrong. Annabel, she realized, was enjoying this. She bowled and knocked down a single pin.

It took the rest of the frame for her to settle down and concentrate on what she was doing. She picked up her final ball and positioned herself. She'd had just enough beer to do this. And when she bowled, the ball went true and straight and she knocked down every single pin and she cheered in delight and then Annabel was behind her, cheering too, and then reaching for her, picking her up at the waist and twirling her around and kissing her deeply.

She tasted the mint of her, the softness of her lips and felt herself respond just as another cheer sounded. Indy pulled back and Annabel dropped her to the floor as they both spun to see Laura, Lars, and Barbara yelling and wolf-whistling.

"Damn it," Annabel muttered.

"We probably should have controlled ourselves better," Indy said.

But her legs were still shaking and she could still feel a puddle of warmth in her belly and suddenly she didn't want to be on camera right now. She spied the plastic beer pitcher, empty now.

"Let me get a refill," she said, grabbing for it and walking off as fast as she could.

She had to cut through a small arcade to make it to the bar. She made it about halfway through the beeping and buzzing and flashing lights before someone caught her from behind.

She didn't have time to scream or even think. The pitcher dropped from her hand and bounced on the carpet and then she was being thrown back against one of the game cabinets and Annabel was pressing against her, kissing her hungrily.

She clung onto Annabel's shirt, her legs wouldn't hold her anymore. She drank her in, feeling the press of her hipbones against her, the bony strength of fingers in her hair, the pulse of a rapid heartbeat in her throat. Until at last, Annabel drew back.

"Sorry," she whispered. "I had to."

Indy grinned. "Can't say that I mind."

"What about another date? One without cameras? Like... an undercover date?" Annabel said, eyes dark with desire.

Indy grinned wider. "Perfect."

Her heart rate hadn't returned to normal by the time that she went back to their lane, filled pitcher in hand. Every time she looked at Annabel her heart skipped a beat and she smiled to herself. But they played out the rest of the game, bidding each other a casual goodbye as they parted in front of the camera.

"Great," Barbara barked. "And that's a wrap. Perfect, ladies. Thank you, you're free to go. And don't forget about that big ending I talked about, eh? I want some ideas there, and I want something big."

But Indy was too busy smiling at Annabel to listen.

CHAPTER TWENTY

The coffee shop was a little more artsy than Annabel would have liked. But it was right up Cassie's street. Cassie looked perfectly at home, her hands cradling a large cup of coffee and her legs crossed as she sank back into an armchair.

"So?" said Cassie.

Annabel crossed her legs, then re-crossed them the other way. She wanted to talk about this, she reminded herself. She needed someone to bounce ideas off. For business, her ideas bounced off Billy. For her personal life? Well, up until a week ago she hadn't actually had a personal life. Cassie had been the one person she could think of to call. The one person that she could open up to. And the one person in exactly the right position to give her the kind of advice she needed.

"So?" she echoed, not sure where to start.

Cassie grinned and pushed her hair behind her ears. "As much as I'm honored to be asked out to coffee, both you and I know that we don't generally have this kind of relationship. Which is fine. I respect you, I respect my husband's taste in friends, and I would never push you into a friendship that was uncomfortable for you."

"Right," said Annabel. She sighed. She kind of needed to take the bull by the horns.

"I'm happy to help you with whatever you need, you know?"

"I know."

"So?" said Cassie again.

"I really like Indy." The words blurted out and sounded stupid as soon as she said them.

To give Cassie her due, she showed no surprise whatsoever. The benefits of talking to a professional, Annabel thought wryly.

"That's fantastic, Annabel."

"Is it really though?" She picked up her own coffee. "I mean, I've wanted to be alone for so long. I'm happy being alone. And now I find that I actually like someone and I'm thinking about changing things, changing the way I am, and I'm not sure I'm okay with that."

Cassie laughed. "Annabel, darling, life is change. That's all it is. If you didn't constantly change, you'd be nowhere. Look at LBN. You're constantly working on it, right? Constantly adding new things? Because if you didn't, it would stagnate. And life is no different."

"I guess."

"This is a good thing, Annabel. You came to me because you want someone to give you permission to change your mind about something, so fine, I give you permission. But you don't actually need it. All you need to do is to decide for yourself and do it. It's really that simple."

Annabel took a breath. Cassie was right, she'd wanted someone's permission. Changing her mind about something as integral to herself as wanting to be alone versus with a partner was a big deal. Yet it hadn't felt that way when it happened. It was like a gleaming realization, seeing Indy, touching her, kissing her and suddenly things fell into place and there she was, happy with another person.

"Not being alone is good, Annabel. As long as you're happy and you're not hurting anyone else, then anything you want is good. Don't doubt your own judgment."

Annabel let out a breath. Knowing something and hearing it from someone else were two different things and she felt better for hearing Cassie.

"So this is the real deal?" Cassie asked.

Annabel nodded. "I think so. I mean, I like her. I don't want to go further than that."

"You've already made a big step," agreed Cassie. "Letting someone else in. That's a big deal. So this whole web series thing, it's going to be for real? No pretending?"

"That's the idea," Annabel said. Which brought her to the second reason she'd asked Cassie out for coffee. "Um, I kind of need to tell Billy all this."

"Agreed. So tell him. It's not like he's going to be angry or anything."

"I'd tell him if I could find him half the time," Annabel said without thinking. Then she calmed a little. "Billy's acting... strange. I know he is, and I suspect you know he is as well."

Cassie sucked at her teeth but said nothing.

"You can't break confidences, I get that," Annabel said. "But if he's concerned because of the company or there's something going on at work, then I feel like I have the right to know."

Cassie took a moment then put her cup down carefully on the table between them. "I can't break confidences. But I can say that Billy is entirely occupied with personal things. This has nothing to do with work."

Annabel nodded. She itched to know what was going on but she wasn't about to press Cassie. "So I should forewarn him about all this." The thought made her feel strange. A little shy, but also proud. She had... a person. She wasn't ready to go with girlfriend yet. Or anything else. But she had a person.

"Tell him," Cassie said. "You'll make him happy."

Annabel nodded.

"So how's all of this sitting with you?" Cassie asked, picking up her coffee again. "Fame and fortune can be difficult to handle."

"I don't look," Annabel confessed. "I don't follow myself on social media, though sometimes I wonder if I should."

"Living in denial can be healthier than some people would have you believe," chuckled Cassie. "Why do you wonder if you should?"

"To see what people are saying about me, to see what information is in the public eye. But I think that it might not be terribly healthy for me to do that."

"I agree," said Cassie. "You don't have the strongest self-image and I feel like this relationship with Indy is bringing you out of yourself. Checking what's online could make you regress."

She'd been bullied enough in person that she didn't need to deal with cyberbullying. She shuddered to think what trolls would be saying.

"If it helps, I'm sure Billy will let you know if anything shocking appears, anything you need to know."

"You're probably right," Annabel said. She finished up the rest of her coffee and put her cup down. "I should get back to the office."

Cassie nodded but then reached out to take Annabel's hand. "I'm proud of you."

"Huh? Why?"

"It takes a strong person to change, a strong person to recognize that just because a belief is long-held doesn't mean that it's correct. This is a big step for you, Annabel. It's a growth step. And this has nothing to do with Indy. The relationship between the two of you may or may not last, that's the nature of relationships, but this lesson you're learning now, that will stay with you forever."

Annabel took a deep breath, surprised at the glint of pain she felt when Cassie mentioned her and Indy breaking up. But she nodded, she heard what was being said and understood it.

"I feel like... like I'm growing up, like I'm becoming a real person," she said, not knowing why she was speaking this aloud.

Cassie smiled back. "You deserve nothing less."

SHE MADE it out of the coffee shop and halfway down the block before someone stepped in front of her.

"Hey, are you her? You are her, aren't you? You're Annabel? Like #IndyAnna? That's you, right?"

Annabel looked at the young woman in front of her, hair up in a sweet ponytail and a wide smile on her face. Cautiously, she nodded.

"I think you're great. I want to be just like you. It's awesome to see a woman like you working in tech. Do you think I could get your autograph? Hold on, I've got a pen here somewhere. No, wait, what about a selfie instead, could we do that?"

Annabel bit back a laugh as the girl hurried to stand beside her and held out her phone to snap the picture.

"Thank you, thanks so much. This is incredible, really awesome, thanks."

"You're very welcome," Annabel said, thinking that maybe this whole fame thing might have its good points. "And you should check out the Women In Tech program, I think it might interest you."

The girl promised to and took off down the street, flicking through her phone to check the pictures she'd just taken.

Helping people. That was an unexpected side effect of agreeing to do this. And one that she liked. Annabel's step was lighter as she walked into her office.

She emailed Billy to arrange lunch with him. Telling him things over a cheeseburger was generally the best way to break any kind of news to him. And then she went through the rest of her inbox.

It was buried in the middle of a collection of office emails. When she read it, her heart started to beat faster and her palms started to sweet and she knew she was grinning like an idiot.

An invitation to interview. She'd just got an invitation to interview for one of the biggest tech think-tanks on the West Coast. She took a deep breath and read through the email again. This was it. This was what she'd been working for, the opportunity that she'd been waiting for.

She checked that the door was closed before she did a happy dance right in the middle of her office. Then she picked up her phone. It wasn't until a voice answered that she realized her first instinct hadn't been to call Billy like she usually did.

"What's up?" Indy asked, the phone line crackling.

CHAPTER TWENTY ONE

Indy placed the beer bottle on the small shelf on the wall and picked up her pool cue.

"Wow, that's a step up from our normal dollar-beer fare," Lucinda said, bending over to make the break.

"That's because we're celebrating," said Indy. She could barely hold the news in. She had to stop herself from just blurting it out.

The call had come just that morning and she'd taken it and thought about it and whichever way she turned it in her mind she couldn't find a flaw. She was no idiot. The world had been trying to tell her something and she'd listened. Not every event was an opportunity. First Annabel, then Dan the stupid agent. But this time, this time she was certain she was onto something.

"Celebrating because you finally kissed Annabel?" Lucinda said, standing up straight again. "I'm solids, by the way."

Indy moved to let her take her shot. "No. Well, yes, always."

"Is now the appropriate time for me to say 'I told you so'?" Lucinda bent over the table again. "Because I feel like it might be."

Indy blew out her cheeks, then shrugged. "Yeah, you know what, I really think it might."

Lucinda didn't take the shot, she stood up instead and came around the table until she could see Indy eyes. Indy shuffled uncomfortably under her gaze.

"Are you about to tick something off your bucket list?"

Indy bit her lip. "Maybe."

"You're actually in love with her?"

"Maybe." Her heart throbbed at the thought of it.

She hadn't wanted to be, hadn't planned on being, but there was something different about Annabel. Something she hadn't had before. And she couldn't put her finger on what it was. She wanted to see her. All the time. She wanted to be in constant contact. She wanted to open her eyes next to her in the morning. She was the first person that Indy had ever imagined herself growing old with.

And it was Annabel.

Strict, cold, not at all what she'd been looking for, Annabel.

"Indy, you're sure?"

"Nothing's sure," Indy said. "We haven't even slept together. But there's something there, some connection. Okay, she'd not what I imagined for myself, but is that so wrong? And yes, she has flaws, of course. But these are flaws that I can live with."

"Are you sure?" Lucinda asked again, tossing her braids over her shoulder. "Because from everything you've said about her if you're not sure then you could do some real damage here. To her as well as to yourself."

"I'm not going to hurt her!"

"I didn't mean to imply that you would deliberately. But she's low on self-confidence and she's opening up to let you in. You need to be careful with people like that. And you need to be careful of yourself as well. You can't just fall in love to tick a box on a list."

Indy scowled. "That's not what this is."

"Alright, alright," said Lucinda, bending to take her shot again. "I just need to check. I just want to make sure you know what you're doing."

"I do. Or at least I think I do. And some congratulations might be nice, you know?" She was getting irritated. Lucinda was picking holes in things, and wasn't this the person who'd told her to wait, to accept someone's flaws, to try something more long term? Okay, she'd promised not to date for three months, but surely this didn't count, did it?

Lucinda took her shot and missed it but before Indy could take her turn she saw a young couple hovering by the wall. Hand in hand they were watching her nervously. Only when she was looking at them did one have the courage to speak.

"You're Indy, aren't you? From #IndyAnna?" one of the girls said nervously.

"Yep," said Indy, making her smile more friendly.

"We just wanted to say that we love you," said the other girl. "And that, well, it's cool. Seeing someone like you. Seeing another lesbian couple, I mean. It makes a change."

And now she was a role model. When had that happened? She smiled and thanked them and they danced off happy with their brush with fame.

"I guess you should get used to that," Lucinda said, sidling up to her. "And I'm sorry."

"Sorry?"

"For raining on your parade. You found something, found someone, and you look happy. I didn't mean to be a bitch about it. I'm happy for you. I just worry, that's all."

"I know you do. And I know that this isn't perfect and that there's a lot to work on, but I feel like I'm starting something here. Something that I might actually finish for once, or see through."

Annabel potentially moving to the West coast, there was one of the imperfections. She'd been truly happy when Annabel had called her, but she knew that a long distance relationship would be more than she could handle. Nothing was set in stone yet though, so she'd told herself to ignore it, to let things happen as they may.

"Then I'm happy for you," said Lucinda.

Indy hugged her, then remembered why they were actually out in the first place. "That isn't the big news," she said, pulling back.

"I'd better have a drink for this." Lucinda grabbed her beer bottle. "Something bigger than finally finding someone who might be a real life girlfriend. I can't even imagine."

Indy elbowed her. "I have an audition."

Slowly, Lucinda put her bottle down. "An audition?"

"It's with a music production company. They're interested in using some of my tracks for an ad campaign they're running. So they've asked me to come in and audition."

Lucinda took a breath. "Indy, are you sure this is for real? After what happened last time?"

"After what happened last time I'm a hell of a lot more careful," Indy said. "The audition is in their offices, which I've already checked out online and they're the real deal. A really real deal. As in I might be able to finally quit the whole call center thing."

Lucinda grinned and picked her beer up again. "That's awesome. And sorry, I can't help being a little protective."

"Not an issue. I was an idiot. And if it makes you feel better I've taken up Amaria from work's offer to teach me some Krav Maga. If anything like what happened with Dan happens again I intend to be fully prepared."

Lucinda clinked her bottle against Indy's. "Life's really looking up, eh?"

"Damn straight."

"You deserve nothing less," said Lucinda. "Now take your shot or I'm winning this game by default."

THE NIGHT was warm enough and she loitered outside the bar waiting for Lucinda to come back from the bathroom so they could make their way home. She was leaning up against the wall when someone spoke to her.

"Just as well things didn't work out between us."

She turned and someone stepped out of the shadows. When she saw who it was, she smiled. "Evelyn!"

"The one and only," Evelyn said, her teeth bright in her face. "And congratulations seem to be in order. You're everywhere.

Tell me, is Annabel really as hot as she looks on video?"

Indy nodded. "She is, I gotta say it."

"Well, I'm glad things are working out for you. You deserve it. You have to be one of the most chivalrous dates I've ever been on. You wouldn't even come back to mine for a night-cap."

"Yeah, I'm old-fashioned that way."

Evelyn grinned again and Indy smiled back. She'd been attracted to the woman for a reason, she remembered. Evelyn was beautiful, tall and statuesque with stunning dark eyes and smooth skin. But she was tapping her fingers on her leg and Indy equally remembered her reason for not taking things further: Evelyn never stopped moving.

"Well, I'll leave you to it," Evelyn said. "It was nice running into you. And I hope this doesn't sound weird, but if you want to give me a call, please do. I know things didn't work out between us, but I could always use a new friend. Especially someone who can play pool."

Indy laughed at that. "Sure thing."

She stepped in and wrapped Evelyn in a hug, slightly drunk and touched by the fact that the woman was being so classy about what had happened between them. Then she let go and stepped back and Evelyn turned to leave and Lucinda came out and then they started walking home.

Later, she played the scene over and over in her mind, trying to figure out where it all went wrong, where her life almost got derailed. But in the moment, all she was thinking about was getting home to a warm bed and dreams of Annabel.

CHAPTER TWENTY TWO

Annabel couldn't imagine her and Billy eating lunch somewhere fancy. It just didn't gel with who they were. Who they had been, she was beginning to realize.

If she was honest with herself she knew that she and Billy had been drifting apart for a while now. Not in a bad way, but in a normal way. Billy was married now, their company was up and running, they were preparing to go separate ways.

Twelve years they'd been friends. Not that they were going to stop being friends. But things were changing. Things had to change. Billy had been the center of her world for a few years there, then that center had moved to accommodate the company. And now, finally, the pay-off was coming, and with it, she knew, came a certain amount of loss.

She was feeling bitter-sweet as Billy hurried into the restaurant, grinning and waving and then sliding himself into a seat.

"Hey there, stranger," she said, grinning right back at him.

"Hey there, yourself," he said. "I'm starving. What are we getting?"

It was a tradition in places like this that they shared at least one thing, a hangover from their poor student days when they couldn't afford much of anything. "I'm thinking about the bacon burger and onion rings," she said.

"Great, I'll get the cheeseburger and fries, then we can share. It's a one for one deal though. One fry for one onion ring."

"Forget it. Five fries per onion ring."

"Two."

"Three, final offer."

Billy looked pained but nodded. "Fine."

Annabel laughed. Billy had always been so easy to be with. It hurt that they were drifting apart, no matter how inevitable it might be. Billy made their order, and when he came back to the table he was looking serious.

"Right, let's get the tough part done, shall we?" he said.

"Hold on, I need to talk to you about something first."

"Annabel—"

"No, this is important." She cleared her throat. "I just want you to know that I know something's going on with you. I get that you might not want to talk about it and I'm fine with that. Your personal life is your own business. I just, I just wanted you to know that I'm here for you. If you need someone to talk to, or if you need someone to cover a meeting or whatever else, I'm here. Don't feel like you need to spill your heart to me, I can help without knowing what's going on."

Billy was flushing and not looking her in the eye. "Thanks, Annabel. That means a lot. Really it does. And you're right, this is personal shit and it won't get in the way of work, okay? I promise you that. I've just got to... I need to deal with this stuff myself first."

"Understood."

She smiled at him and a waiter brought over two plastic trays. They emptied out their fries and onion rings onto one tray, pushing it to the center of the table.

"So," Billy started again.

Annabel held out a hand. Best to get all this over with at once. "There's more." She unwrapped her burger. "I've been offered an interview at ILB."

Billy's eyebrows shot up. "The think-tank?"

"Where else?"

"Jesus, that's amazing news. It's incredible, congratulations."

"I might not get the job."

"What are you talking about?" He was animated now and she could see he was truly happy for her. "Of course you'll get it. You're Annabel Taylor. Everyone's going to want you. Especially once we sell LBN."

"I think it's about time to start real negotiations," Annabel said. "We need to make this real. We don't want to hold off for long enough for our stock to drop."

"Agreed. I've already put feelers out. But I'll let it be known that we're entertaining offers." Billy held out his paper soda cup. "We've really done it. Achieved exactly what we said we would."

Grinning, Annabel tapped her cup against his. "Did you ever doubt it?"

"With you? No," said Billy.

"I'll be off to the West coast and you can buy that yacht and get started on all those kids you want," said Annabel.

Billy's smile dropped a little. "Annabel, there's something—"

"Still not done," she said, holding her burger in both hands. "There's something else you need to know. It's not major, but, um, but you should know." She cleared her throat again. Jesus, this felt weird. "Um, Indy and I, we, um, we're kind of..." She didn't know how to complete that sentence. Kind of what? "Well, we're sort of together," she finished lamely.

Billy didn't look terribly surprised. If anything, he looked sad. "Nothing major? That's pretty major, Annabel."

"I guess." His sadness was catching and she didn't know why. The air seemed heavier and harder to breathe.

"So that algorithm wasn't as flawed as you thought, huh?" Billy said, obviously trying to lighten the mood.

Annabel rolled her eyes. "I don't believe in all that bullshit. You know that. The algorithm is as good as the information that it's fed. There's no such thing as a soulmate. It's ridiculous to think that there's only one person in the world for each of us. Not to mention statistically improbable."

But as she was talking she could see that Billy wasn't really listening, that he had other things on his mind. And that despite his weak attempt at a joke the atmosphere was still darker by the moment.

"What?" she asked, feeling a flutter of panic in her stomach.

"Cassie told me," said Billy. "She told me about you and Indy. And she told me..." He sighed and bit his lip before turning to look her in the eye. "She told me that I should tell you if anything happened you should know about. That you don't follow social media so I should keep you in the loop."

She was colder now. Colder on the inside. "Right."

Billy blinked, tilting his head a little. "Is that true, Annabel? Do you want to hear what people are saying? Do you really want to know? Because, honestly, I think that sometimes ignorance is bliss. Sometimes it's just better to go on with your life without knowing something. Even if that thing's huge and life-changing and un-ignorable. Maybe it's better to be in the dark for as long as you can."

Her stomach was filled with tremors now. She was starting to be afraid. "Tell me."

"Annabel, I really wish I didn't have to. I wish I didn't have to be the one to do this. I'm so sorry."

"Just tell me." Her voice was quiet, barely there, as though she couldn't trust herself to speak.

Billy nodded. He wiped his hands carefully with a napkin and reached into his pocket, pulling out his phone.

"Tell me," she said again.

"It's Indigo." Billy clicked through something on his phone. "She, uh, well, you guys are together but..." Another sigh, bigger this time. Finally, he just turned his phone over to her. "This is all over the gossip sites and social media right now."

She didn't touch the phone. She stared at the swirl of colors on the screen, trying to make sense of them, trying to understand what was going on. Then she sat back, pushed her food away.

"It's okay, Annabel. It's okay. I'm here. I should never have pushed you to do this. I shouldn't—"

"This isn't your fault," she said, calmer now that at least she knew what was happening. "It's not your fault at all. It's mine. I should have been more careful, should have protected myself better."

"I don't think you of all people could be accused of not protecting yourself," Billy said gently. "If anything, you protect yourself too much."

"No, no, I make mistakes just like anyone else does."

Billy nodded. "What do you want me to do?"

She thought about all the consequences, thought about the plans that could be ruined, the hearts that could be broken, and it was so overwhelming that she could barely grasp what was happening. One thing at a time. One step at a time.

"If it's alright with you, I think I'm going to take the afternoon off," she said.

Billy nodded. "It's fine, of course."

"I'll tell you tomorrow morning what I think we should do. If that's okay?" She checked again, knowing that this impacted the company and Billy just as much as it affected her.

"It's fine, Annabel. You do what you need to do. I'll take care of everything else. It's fine."

"No press releases, no comments, nothing until tomorrow morning, okay?"

"Not a problem." He eked out a small smile. "Mystery always sells better anyway."

She pushed her chair back. "I'm going to leave now."

She needed to be home, she needed to be alone, she needed to be in a world where she hadn't just seen what she'd seen.

A photo. Slightly grainy. A face that was distinctly Indy's, her arms around a woman. Another woman. A tall, beautiful black woman. Indy in the arms of another woman.

Her stomach flipped and she knew she was going to throw up.

CHAPTER TWENTY THREE

Indy's heart was in her boots. There was a brisk breeze and she tried to look as inconspicuous as possible but she was cold and... and she obviously didn't dress like she belonged in a place like this. She'd pressed the buzzer until her finger hurt. Now, finally, a man was opening the building door. Putting on a spurt of speed she managed to catch the door just before it closed again and slipped through it.

She'd checked the LBN offices first, obviously. But the receptionist had said Annabel wasn't there and that, more than anything else, scared her. Annabel not working. Three o'clock in the afternoon and Annabel wasn't in her office.

So she'd taken a moment, centered herself, tried to put herself in Annabel's place. And then she'd settled on the apartment. Feeling betrayed, feeling emotional, feeling hurt, the only place that Annabel would be was the apartment. The place where she felt safe.

The place where she was refusing to answer calls, unlock the building door, or respond to texts.

But Indy wasn't having this. She wasn't about to be some stupid heroine in a romance movie, one that walks away because the hero won't talk to her. She was damned if she was letting Annabel go without a fight.

Which was how she ended up banging on the door.

"Let me in."

There was a long pause and she considered banging again.

"Go away."

Finally. A channel of communication.

"No, I won't go away, Annabel. I know you're hurt, but I need to speak to you. And these games are below you. Open the door and let us talk like adults."

Another pause. "I don't know if I can."

"If you can talk to me?"

"If I can talk to anyone. Without, you know, without crying."

"That's what you're afraid of? Afraid that you might cry?" Afraid that she'd show any kind of emotion. Indy felt a stab of pity for a young, bullied girl, one who'd learned fast not to show what the bullying did to her.

"Maybe."

Indy made her voice as gentle as she could. "This isn't what you think, Annabel. Please let me in. I'd like to explain myself. I'll leave the second you tell me to leave."

A final long pause and then the lock clicked and the door opened.

Annabel was dressed in black lounge pants and a white shirt. Her face was pale, her hair up, her regular make-up just a little smudged. A pang of desire went through Indy just from the sight of her.

"Thank you," she said. "Can I come in? This is a huge misunderstanding, I promise you."

Annabel didn't move.

Indy took a deep breath. "Okay, you don't let people in. You don't trust people. And all of this just proves to you why you shouldn't trust someone. Right this second I can't think of a single reason why you should trust me. But I'm asking you to do it anyway. I'm asking you to give me a chance, based on your past experience with me."

Finally, Annabel moved and Indy came inside.

"It's not what it seems?"

"No," said Indy. "Not at all. This is... this is the media at its worst. This is the flip side of that fun marketing project we've been doing. Not all publicity is good publicity, you know that."

"But—"

"But nothing, Annabel. I get how this looks." She was getting a little angry now, and had to force herself to lower her voice. "Look me in the eye and tell me that you honestly think I'd do something like this to you? That I'd cheat on you so stupidly and publicly."

Annabel stepped in closer and Indy felt the heat of her and then she was shaking her head. "You wouldn't. I guess I know that. I suppose I should have called you first, talked to you first. But I got scared. Which sounds silly."

"It doesn't sound silly."

Annabel smiled a little. "Yes, it does. All of this makes me look like a crazy, jealous, weird-o. But I'm not used to letting people in. I'm really not. And... and why didn't you tell me?"

"Because I was at work," Indy sighed. "No phones allowed at my desk. I only just found out myself when I got Evelyn's text."

"Evelyn?"

"The woman in the photo. She's a friend. Not even. We've met all of three times. I was at a bar playing pool with my room-mate last night and I ran into Evelyn on the way out. We chatted for a couple of minutes, we hugged goodbye. End of story."

"Ironic," said Annabel, walking over to the couch. "We spend so long fooling the world and pretending to be in a relationship, and then when we finally decide to give things a try, the world tries to fool us right back again."

Indy went to sit next to her. "Yeah, I guess. I didn't mean for this to happen, you know? I talked to Laura. She's going to set something up with Evelyn. An interview or something. So that all of this doesn't affect the web series, or business or anything."

"Is it supposed to be this... disconcerting?" Annabel asked.

"Being in a relationship?"

"I just..." Annabel slumped back. "I knew you didn't do it, didn't kiss her. As soon as I really had a chance to think about it,

I knew. I mean, you asked me to find you love, that was my part of the deal, so what were the chances that you'd found it yourself in the few weeks since you asked me? And you've kept your word about everything so far. Once I'd calmed down, I knew it was all bullshit. But..."

"But you couldn't help feeling afraid."

"Right. Afraid that next time it might be real, or that this really won't work out, or, I don't know. It seemed safer not to let you in. Sorry about that. I always felt safer alone."

Indy nodded. "I get it. I get that it's hard sharing your life with someone else. It's not exactly a picnic for me either. I... I have problems committing to things. To people. I see one sign of a flaw and I want to run away."

Annabel turned her blue eyes on her. "So coming here was kind of a big deal, huh? Coming here and facing the problem rather than just running from it?"

"Well, we are kind of famous now, so running away isn't as easy as it used to be," said Indy, smiling.

At last, Annabel laughed. "It is hard, isn't it?"

Indy let out a breath. "It's hard. But hopefully worth it. I mean, if you still want..."

Annabel reached out and cupped her face. "If I still want to take the risk? It's not like I have much choice, like you said, we're pretty famous now."

And then Annabel's lips were closer and closer until they were kissing and for a second Indy could forget about everything. For a long time, they sat, kissing and touching and not talking. The light in the apartment grew grey.

"There's something I haven't told you," Indy said finally, lazily, the words sounding strange after such a long silence.

"A secret?" murmured Annabel.

"Not exactly," smiled Indy. She had to be honest, she had to tell her. "I have an audition. For a production company here in the city. They might want to use some of my music."

"That's wonderful," Annabel said. But a shadow had passed over her face.

"You don't sound like it's wonderful."

"I just— I just wonder what will happen to us, is all. Me interviewing for a job in California, you getting your break here in the city. It feels like the world is against us."

Indy took a breath but nodded. "It might feel like that. Maybe it is like that. I don't know. I can't tell the future, Annabel."

"So, what do we do?"

There was a moment there when Indy could have stopped everything. When she could have walked away. Except Annabel's eyes were such a dark blue and her lips were so soft and the evening light had begun to glint in her hair. And as much as she knew that this wasn't perfect, perhaps that was what made it perfect in the first place.

"We ignore the flaws," she said. "That's what Lucinda says. She says I have to learn to ignore the flaws, to live with them. So perhaps that's what we need to do. Whatever happens will happen. We can only control the here and now."

"That sounds... irresponsible."

But Annabel's voice was close to her ear and her breath was tickling and she didn't sound like she minded being irresponsible at all. Indy pulled back just a fraction.

"Unless you really want to stop this? Unless you don't want to take the risk?"

Annabel's hand was brushing along her arm, the light touch of her fingertips making Indy's skin prickle with wanting. "We're really not suited, are we?" she murmured. "But perhaps that's what makes us so suited, the fact that neither one of us is what the other is looking for. Neither one of us is the unachievable ideal that we've set for ourselves."

Indy's mouth was dry. It took her two attempts to speak. "So, shall we be irresponsible?" she asked.

Annabel looked at her with heavy-lidded eyes. For a brief second Indy's heart stopped beating. Then she nodded. "Let's."

CHAPTER TWENTY FOUR

Indy's hands were on her waist and Annabel let herself be led into the kiss, let lips glide down over her neck, let the smell of Indy and the taste of her consume her. And then she was moving closer still, the small couch creaking slightly as she did.

She let herself touch Indy, let her fingers roam over her body. She wanted this, truly did, could feel the heat building up inside her. But. Something was stopping her, holding her back.

"Indy..." The word was more of a sigh than anything.

Indy lifted her head. "Mmm?"

"I'm afraid."

She knew what was coming next, the question that Indy would ask. She felt stupid, her stomach shaking and her hands shaking and desire deep in her stomach.

"Of what?"

"Everything." She hadn't known until she said it that she was going to honest. "I'm afraid of breaking you."

Indy threw back her head and laughed. "I'm a lot more robust than I look."

Annabel felt herself blush and Indy's hand tightened on the curve of her waist. "It's, um, it's been a while."

"Almost two years for me," responded Indy.

Annabel blinked. "Really? I would have thought..."

"Then you would have thought wrong. I don't do this with everyone. I do this with hardly anyone. But I want to do it with you."

She could see from the look on Indy's face that she was being honest and her fears receded a little. She nodded. "Okay. But… slowly, maybe?"

"As slow as you like," Indy said, dipping her head once again to pepper the soft skin of Annabel's neck with tiny kisses.

Annabel felt her skin bristle with electricity. Indy's kisses moved down further, reaching her collarbone and then further still until without thinking about it, without considering it for a second, she could stand it no longer and she pulled off her own shirt, giving Indy full access.

"Jesus," Indy said.

"No, just me," said Annabel, then cursed herself for joking at a time like this. A bad joke as well, not even something that funny.

But Indy laughed anyway and teased a finger under the edge of Annabel's bra. "Can I?"

Entranced at the thought of Indy's mouth on her breasts, Annabel nodded and Indy carefully unclasped the black lace.

"Jesus," she said again, before lowering her head.

Annabel groaned as Indy took a nipple into her mouth. Soft sucking at first, swirling her tongue around the hardness until she started to lick with more force and a direct line of pleasure shocked all the way down to Annabel's center.

She could feel her own wetness, could feel her underwear sticking to her. Her pulse had quickened and her heartbeat was erratic and her breath was coming faster and still Indy licked and sucked.

She tangled her fingers in Indy's soft, blonde hair and pulled her in closer. In response, Indy sucked harder until Annabel moaned.

"Please."

Indy raised her head. "Please?"

"Please. I want this. I want you. Please."

Indy's hands were on her waist and Annabel arched her back,

letting that mouth take her breast again and feeling the need build up in her. She thought about asking again but couldn't form words. She pressed herself against Indy's tongue until finally, agonizingly slowly, Indy began to kiss down her stomach.

Thumbs were stroking against her hipbones and Indy's face was getting closer to her wetness and Annabel couldn't help but thrust upward with her hips.

Indy looped her thumbs under the waistband of Annabel's pants. She looked up, turquoise eyes shining. "May I?"

Still struck dumb, Annabel nodded, lifting herself a little so that Indy could pull down her pants and her underwear in one smooth motion. She was bared now, completely naked and vulnerable and Indy was still fully dressed and she should feel uncomfortable. But she didn't. She was too busy concentrating on the feeling building up inside her, too busy hoping that Indy was going to do what she thought she was going to do and yet afraid of it as well.

Indy was still looking at her and Annabel forced herself to look back, not to turn away or to close her eyes as Indy's hands parted her thighs and laid her completely open.

"Watch me," Indy said, mouth swollen and eyes hot. "Watch me, trust me."

Annabel nodded as Indy lowered her head, never breaking eye contact.

She shuddered as Indy's tongue flickered out and tickled her. And then groaned as Indy's head lowered further, the full length of her tongue beginning to brush against her.

Blood was rushing faster and faster through her veins. She felt the pressure building up inside her and knew she couldn't wait long, couldn't hold off no matter how much she wanted this. And still Indy stared up at her, still they were in contact, still she knew that there was someone else there. She couldn't disappear into her own head like she normally did.

Indy's movements grew faster and faster and Annabel's breath came faster and faster and it was like a flood being held back until finally, inevitably, the dam broke.

She kept her eyes open as long as she could, seeing Indy's eyes widen as she began to buck her hips and surrender to her climax. But then she had to screw her eyes shut as the feelings became too much, too strong, and wave after wave rushed over her.

She came back to earth slowly. The only sound was the hoarseness of her breathing.

"Here," Indy said. "Just relax for a moment."

Annabel lay back, snuggling into the corner of the couch, reclining as her narrowed eyes watched Indy undress.

Indy's skin was pale, almost luminous in the grey light. Her breasts were high, her hips curved and Annabel ached to touch her, but didn't dare.

"You won't break me," Indy said, crawling up onto the couch. "I promise you won't."

But Annabel couldn't quite bring herself to believe it. Until Indy turned her back on her, sliding between her still open legs so that her warm back was pressed against Annabel's breasts.

"Touch me," Indy said.

Hands shaking, Annabel allowed herself to run her fingers up Indy's arms and then down, pausing momentarily before she was cupping breasts that were deceptively full. Indy pushed herself back, increasing their contact so Annabel pinched lightly at her nipples, feeling them wrinkled and hard against her fingertips.

"Jesus," Indy said, her voice a soft moan.

Annabel laughed a little, confidence growing as she let her hand wander further down. She drifted over the curve of Indy's waist, the hardness of her hipbones.

"I want you," Indy said. "Please."

With permission given, she let her hands go even lower, feeling the wiry softness of Indy's hair, and then, suddenly, the stickiness of her thighs. Indy groaned and parted her legs and Annabel reached to touch her.

It was almost like touching herself. Indy was pushed up against her and Annabel felt her sex rubbing against Indy's back even as she touched Indy and found her wet and ready and waiting, swollen beneath her fingers.

"Harder," Indy muttered, her breath already coming in gasps. "Harder."

Annabel obliged, letting her fingers slip in Indy's wetness, coming up to circle around the hard swollen center of her until Indy's hips were moving and Annabel felt herself grinding against the base of Indy's back, her own breath coming faster again.

"Harder," Indy said again. "Harder. Harder."

There was a throbbing under her fingers, and an equal throbbing in her own center. Annabel thrust herself up, letting Indy's movements rub against her even as her own fingers were coaxing Indy closer and closer to the edge.

"Come for me," she whispered. Though what she meant was let me come, press yourself shivering against me and let me feel it until we both jump over that cliff.

Indy groaned and her hips bucked harder and then she cried out just as Annabel pushed hard against her and then they were both flying, shivering and trembling. Annabel clasped Indy tightly to her, not believing what was happening but letting the glow of it surround her anyway until her breath started to come again in gasps then sighs.

Indy laid back, heavy on her now.

"That's never happened to me before," Annabel said, half-embarrassed at the admission but proud enough of what happened to want Indy to know that it was something special. "I've never come with someone before like that."

Indy squirmed, turned so that they were looking at each other. She looked sleepy, still flushed and lips swollen. "Worth taking the risk?" she asked.

Annabel laughed, holding Indy's body tight against hers. "I'd say yes, wouldn't you?"

"I think there's something to this 'ignoring the problems until they all go away' thing," Indy agreed. She leaned up kissed Annabel's mouth and nibbled at her lip.

"And there's a lot to be said for not being alone," Annabel said, the heat of Indy's skin against hers so unbelievably soft.

"And maybe algorithms aren't as bad as I've always thought," Indy said, reaching around so that she was pulling Annabel to her again.

"Again?" Annabel said, heart already starting to pound.

"Unless you're tired?" asked Indy, face all innocence.

Annabel laughed. "Why don't we take this to the bedroom?"

But in the end, they only made it as far as the corridor before the whole cycle started all over again.

CHAPTER TWENTY FIVE

Indy leaned her guitar against the edge of the desk. The woman in front of her noted something down then nodded, bending to speak quietly to the man next to her. Indy gulped. She'd done her best, she knew that she was good. But was she good enough?

Finally, the man gave a firm nod, stood up, smiled at Indy, and left the room. That had to be a good sign, right? The woman turned back. Indy was damned if she could remember her name. She'd been so nervous walking in that she'd blanked out everything up until the moment she picked up her guitar.

But the woman was smiling.

"We're impressed."

Indy's heart started to beat again and she wiped her sweaty hands on her pants. "Thank you."

"And we're interested," the woman continued. "Very interested. I don't know how much has been explained to you. But what we'd like to do is record a couple of tracks to use for an advertising campaign. Should that take off, then we'd commit to producing a full album."

"Um, that sounds... fantastic." What else could she say?

The woman smiled. "I'm glad you agree. However, there is one small sticking point."

Indy didn't dare ask.

"You are one half of #IndyAnna, aren't you?"

A breath. "Yes." There was no point in denying it.

The woman smiled again. "That's a good thing and a bad thing. We're liking that you're already out there, that you're making a name for yourself. That makes our job easier. In fact, that's part of the reason we were interested in you."

Well, at least this stupid dating show had been good for something. Not that she regretted meeting Annabel. Not at all. Her core ached thinking about the night they'd spent together. What she was getting tired of though was being constantly filmed. She'd enjoy having her privacy back, at least to some extent.

"We are aware, however, that you're still filming the web series."

"Is that a problem?" Indy asked. "Because we're wrapping things up at the end of next week so there shouldn't be any conflict."

"That's great," the woman smiled again. Indy was beginning to think that smiling was just her default response. "We're more worried about appearances though. We can't afford to be linked to any... scandal."

"Hey, that stuff in the papers was—"

"Was unfortunate and untrue, we know," the woman smiled. "However, we can't know what will happen in the next week or so. So we're happy to extend you an offer on the contingency that nothing... untoward happens whilst you're filming."

"No more scandals."

"No more scandals," the woman agreed.

It seemed fair. And her heart was beating so fast it sounded like a rhythm section and her legs were starting to shake. This was really happening. She was really about to get her break. After so long it seemed almost impossible.

She wanted so badly to be happy. She was happy. But there was that little splinter of sadness as well, buried deep down inside. Because as much as she wanted to ignore all the flaws in her relationship with Annabel, this might be one that was way beyond ignoring. If she took this job and Annabel took the one in California, what then?

They wouldn't be able to ignore that distance for long, would they?

❋ ❋ ❋

Annabel sat next to Indy and tried hard to keep her hands to herself. She found herself grinning every time their eyes met and she wanted to kiss her. No, she wanted to throw her down on the table and have her wicked way with her. Highly inappropriate given that they were currently in a diner with Lars, Laura and Barbara in attendance.

"We need to talk about that big ending," Barbara said, as a huge milkshake was placed in front of her. "We wrap next week and I want this decided. We need a big bang. Anyone come up with anything?"

Annabel was only half-listening, her attention firmly on Indy's hand, which had just slid across the bench seat and started brushing against her thigh.

"I, uh, I was thinking about it," Laura offered.

Maybe Lars was mute. Had she ever heard Lars speak? She tried to think and was sure that she must have done. Yet it was only Laura that she ever remembered having any input. Lars seemed happier with his camera, hiding behind it.

Indy's hand stroked her own and Annabel grinned.

"Well, spit it out, girl," Barbara said.

"It might sound silly," said Laura. "But I've been doing some research. Um, research. Mostly watching TV."

"In our business, that's research," Barbara said, slurping at her milkshake.

"Right. So. Most dating shows have one kind of ending. I'm not saying it's something we should do, I'm just saying that it might be an expectation of the genre, that's all. You see, most dating shows, well, they end with one thing."

Barbara scowled and it was Indy that broke in.

"With a proposal."

"Exactly," Laura said, with a grin.

Annabel froze. A proposal.

"It seems a little cliché. I'm not sold on a proposal per se," Barbara mused. "However, yes, a big gesture does seem called for. Perhaps a 'be my girlfriend' proposal, rather than a 'be my wife' proposal. That could work. Something definitive, so that viewers know what's going to happen to the two of you. Yes. I like it."

"I—" began Annabel.

But then she became even more aware of Indy's warmth next to her, the scent of her, the memory of her skin, her touch. And she shut up. What could she say? If she refused to do it then Indy would surely be upset. More to the point, did she really want to refuse? She had no idea, she'd given this no thought at all.

Ignore the flaws, Indy had said. Which was a great plan for the short term. But in the longer term? Who knew? She felt her stomach start to shake. What did she want here?

"Are we settled then?" Barbara said.

There was no real disagreement, which Barbara took to mean they all agreed and then it was too late, they were all off to the restaurant for a quickly filmed dinner date.

All through dinner, Annabel watched Indy's mouth, the way it moved when she spoke, the softness of her lips. They discussed inconsequential things, but she couldn't take her eyes off the woman.

Should they make things more formal?

The idea terrified her. But then, something else had terrified her as well. Those few minutes when she'd thought that Indy was with someone else, after she first saw the photos. Right then she'd been terrified. Afraid that she'd lost her, afraid that her one chance of happiness was gone.

Being with Indy did make her happy. Not something she would have expected. And not something that had ever happened with anyone else. Which led her to believe that this might just be her one chance.

At the end of their filmed date they both left separately, meeting up around the corner from the restaurant, away from the prying eyes of the cameras. But Annabel had too much still to think about to discuss what had happened.

Indy squeezed her hand. "I really should go. I have to get up early in the morning."

The touch sent Annabel's pulse soaring. She leaned in, touched Indy's lips with her own, felt the movement of Indy's body responding, pushing against her. But she pulled herself back. Space was not a bad thing.

"Understood," she whispered.

Indy stroked her face with one hand and then they walked toward the metro together, not speaking at all.

SHE'D KNOWN that the call was coming. She'd spent two hours one afternoon four days ago on video call with the company. And she'd known that they'd let her know one way or the other. Okay, she hadn't expected the call so late. But then, ILB were on West coast time.

She paused before she picked the phone up, thinking that maybe not knowing would be better than knowing. She took one last breath and then picked up.

"Ms. Taylor? Declan Wright here from ILB."

"Yes, speaking."

"I won't beat around the bush. We were very impressed with your interview, and we'd like to offer you the position."

She stopped dead in the middle of the street outside her apartment building. This. This was what it had all been for. This was the golden ring, the cigar, the dream.

"Of course, you're welcome to come and tour our facilities before committing to the position, we'd completely understand that. But in essence, the job is yours if you want it."

The night was cool and her breath was coming fast and there was nothing that she wanted more than this job.

Or she thought there wasn't.

Right up until she opened her mouth to accept and found that the words wouldn't come out.

Yes, she wanted the job. But she wanted Indy as well. Maybe more.

And a week from now she'd know exactly how Indy felt about her because it would all be on film, the stupid proposal that wasn't really a proposal. And maybe she should wait just a heartbeat to balance all these things and decide what she really, truly wanted in life. She swallowed.

"I'd love to tour your facilities," she said. "Would the week after next work?"

"Perfect," chuckled Wright. "We'll be looking forward to your visit."

Annabel hung up. She hadn't not accepted the position.

But she hadn't accepted it either.

And she had some serious thinking to do.

CHAPTER TWENTY SIX

It was easy to fall into habits. Like Indy spending every second night in her apartment. Something that a few months ago, Annabel would have found disconcerting and strange and unpleasant. Like having someone to turn to and laugh with. Like having someone to touch.

And as the week wore on, she pushed her decisions further and further away. Until it was the day and there was no more time to decide.

Another habit was meeting up before the series shot. This time, they were all in a cafe, Annabel and Indy with coffees in front of them, Lars and Laura getting final instructions from Barbara.

Eventually, Barbara sent the blonde look-alikes on their way to get started, and turned to Annabel and Indy.

"Alright, ladies, this has been discussed. We're going for a nice wrap-up here. What I want is for a sort of proposal, a girlfriend proposal if you will. I don't care which of you does it, I don't care if you get down on one knee or not. I don't want it scripted. All I care about is making good TV. Are we okay with that?"

They hadn't discussed it. After that first day, the whole proposal idea had become yet another one of those flaws that had been ignored. And Annabel honestly didn't know what she was going to do or say. She could feel Indy's presence next to her though.

"I'll be going then," Barbara said, not even waiting for their agreement. "Give me ten minutes or so, then I want one of you coming in first. Annabel, you. Give her a few minutes, then you come in, Indy. I want a little time to shoot Annabel alone so we can put a voice-over of her thoughts onto that section."

Again, she didn't wait for agreement or any sign that they understood, she just left. Someone held the door open for her as she went, and Annabel didn't recognize who until he stepped into the coffee shop himself.

"Billy, what are you doing here?"

"Do you think I'd miss your final episode?" he said with a grin.

He'd missed everything else, she thought. But she remembered that she'd promised to help and that he was dealing with his own personal stuff. "You haven't actually met Indy, have you?"

"I've seen her face a million times," Billy said. He leaned down and gave Indy a hug. "And this is going to seem really rude, but do you think I could steal Annabel from you for maybe five minutes?"

Indy grinned. "No probs, I need a refill anyway. Can I get you something?"

"Decaf would be great."

He waited until Indy left before sitting down. "So, there's something you need to see."

"What?"

"An offer."

She could see from the look on his face that this was the one, this was what they'd been waiting for. For just a second she remembered how all of this had started, Billy with his thick curls desperately trying to persuade her to use her coding skills for his new dating app idea. It hurt a little to know that something was ending. But something was beginning too, she had to think of that.

Billy held out his phone, a number typed on the screen. She

looked at it, looked at Billy, looked back at the phone and then had to close her eyes against a wave of dizziness.

"I know," Billy said. "I know."

"That's..." She couldn't even finish the sentence.

Billy sat back in his chair. "Now for the real question. Do we take it?"

She opened her eyes, saw Billy watching her, and couldn't read his mind. She'd thought that she knew what he wanted, but could she be sure? She licked dry lips. "What do you think?"

"I asked first."

She took a deep breath. "It's something we should strongly consider," she said carefully.

His mouth twitched like he was holding in a grin. "Consider?" he said. "Or take?"

He wasn't going to let this go, he wasn't going to let her off the hook. Fine. She'd go first. "I think we should take it."

Billy slumped in his chair. "Thank God. I thought you might tell me to wait. Yes, yes we should take it. There's no point being greedy. This is all we need and more."

She nodded, feeling faint again at the thought of the figure Billy had shown her. "We're really doing this?"

"We've really done this," Billy said, smile wider and wider. "I'll get the process started. This is it. We've made it, Annabel."

They were suddenly quiet, like the reality of it all was dawning on them. And then Indy came back.

"Shouldn't you be heading out?" she asked, as she put Billy's coffee down.

Annabel jumped up. Of course. This one last loose end to tie up. And she'd given zero thought in the last ten minutes to what she was about to do. Or not do. But there was no time now.

She'd just have to decide in the moment.

❅ ❅ ❅

"You look happy," Indy said, settling back into her own chair.

Billy leaned in to take his cup. "Can you keep a secret?"

"One of my finer skills," she answered. She liked him. She'd heard enough about him, of course, but she hadn't been expecting someone quite so charming. If she was honest, she'd have expected someone a little, well, nerd-ier.

"We just got an offer for the company. A big offer."

Her eyes widened. "Are you taking it?"

"That was always the plan," Billy said, crossing his legs. "And you know Annabel, there's always a plan."

Just how well did she know Annabel though, that was the question? Well enough to want to take part in this stupid fake proposal idea? Well enough to actually want to commit to her? Well enough to potentially walk out on the first great opportunity she'd had in the music world?

Or well enough to live thousands of miles apart and watch their relationship crumble?

"I guess this is what she wants," she said, mildly.

Billy shook his head and laughed. "You know, she never believed in any of this? Oh, the business part, sure. But the romance part, the soulmate part, that's not Annabel."

"The algorithm is hers," Indy pointed out.

"Yes, it is. But that was just a mathematical exercise for Annabel. Nothing more, nothing less. She's never believed in any of the lovey-dovey stuff." He eyed her over his cup. "And then you come along."

He made that sound almost like a bad thing. "People are allowed to change their minds."

"Maybe," Billy said. "But only if it's really a change of mind. Not if it's simply a distraction. It's easy for you to say that now, because you only know Annabel now. But before... You weren't there."

He didn't sound nasty, not really. Maybe this was more like a warning.

"You weren't there for the long nights, the struggle to pay rent, the nights where we had to find a couch to sleep on. You didn't see the sacrifices that Annabel had to make. And as much as she might say she always wanted to be alone, she never had a chance to have things any other way. She put everything into building this company. All with one end goal in sight. Selling up, getting the cash, and moving out to California to be surrounded by the kind of programmers and coders that have inspired and challenged her."

Indy took this in. "And you're afraid that she might deny herself that reward to please me." It wasn't a question.

Billy shook his head. "I know love. I have love. I'm the last person that would deny someone as special as Annabel the chance to have what I have. Honestly, I mean that. But I would like you to be careful. Because I'm not sure that you really realize what's at stake here. This is the beginning of something for Annabel."

"And maybe she shouldn't carry old baggage along with her."

Billy ran his hand through his curls. "Not what I meant. Jesus. I'm coming off as kind of an asshole here, aren't I?"

Indy shrugged. "Kind of."

Billy sighed. "Just… Please be careful with her, that's all. Please look after my Annabel. Because she's not always great at looking after herself."

She stared at him for a long minute before nodding. "I have to go."

"Good luck."

What was she going to do? She had no idea. She needed to do what was best for Annabel and she didn't know what that was. Except she did, really, didn't she? She'd chosen to keep the news of the successful audition to herself. She hadn't told Annabel. Because she knew in the end what she really had to do.

CHAPTER TWENTY SEVEN

It was ridiculous. Completely ridiculous. She felt ridiculous even just thinking about it. But as the moment approached, she was more and more sure of what she was going to do.

The date was a sweet one. Cakes and champagne in an intimate little patisserie that Laura had somehow found. Lars and Laura were bouncing around, filming and taking pictures, and Barbara was standing in the corner, arms crossed, watching grimly to ensure nothing terrible happened.

"Favorite kind of cake?" Indy asked her.

Turquoise eyes and generous mouth and the touch of her hands. How could she do without that? Now that she'd tasted what was to be had, she couldn't go back to the way she was before. Or at least she didn't want to.

"Vanilla, obviously," she said.

Indy rolled her eyes. "Seriously? Literally every other person in the world would say chocolate."

Annabel shrugged. "I'm not every other person in the world."

Indy held her eyes for a long moment. "I know," she said, finally. And perhaps she sounded just a little sad.

She had to step out of her comfort zone. She had to own the fact that she'd changed her mind, that she'd been wrong. She had to be the one to ask, because she was the one that needed it. She was the loner, the one that had never wanted anyone, so it was important that she be the one to invite Indy formally into her life.

It had to be that way.

She could debate it all she wanted, and there were plenty of arguments both pro and con. But if she ignored the flaws, ignored the stupid logistics of things, then there was one truth. She wanted to be with Indy. That was it. That was all.

Indy was bringing a fork full of cake to her mouth and Annabel could barely breathe with the thought of what she was doing. From the corner of her eye she saw Lars sweeping around with his camera and Barbara glaring at her, daring her to go ahead and do it.

"Indy."

Her voice came out as a croak. Jesus. She was sweating like she'd run a marathon and her heart was about to beat out of her chest. She cleared her throat and tried again.

"Indy."

The turquoise eyes looked up at her. "Yes?"

She cleared her throat again. What was she supposed to say? She looked over Indy's shoulder, silently begging someone, anyone for help here. Laura took pity on her and mouthed the word 'girlfriend,' as though Annabel had forgotten just what she was supposed to be doing here.

"Indy," she tried yet again. She looked down at the table. "I love being with you." It was easier without the eye contact. Easier when she didn't have to remember that she was being filmed. "I spent a long time thinking that I should be alone. And then I met you. You made me realize that there was more to life than what I had. You made me want more. And now that this dating journey is coming to an end, there's something that I really need to ask you."

She dared a glance up and saw that Indy was pale, her eyes wide, that her mouth was slightly open as though she wanted to interrupt. Annabel swallowed. Had she misread this? Had something changed? It was too late to stop things now.

"Would you make this official and be my girlfriend?" The words rushed out of her mouth so fast that she couldn't possibly stop them.

And then there was silence. A big silence that encompassed the entire room and Annabel could hear her own heartbeat and the glass shell she'd surrounded herself with was starting to crack and she'd never been so scared in all her life.

Indy looked down.

"Yes," she said.

Annabel's head swirled as she heard the word.

* * *

She'd been warned. No more scandals. Making waves on camera would mean no shot with the music production company. But it was more than that, in the end. There was something that she couldn't do, she'd decided. She couldn't do this on film. She had to fulfill her end of the deal and there was no way in hell that she was going to humiliate Annabel any more than she'd already done.

She waited. Waited while Lars and Laura and Barbara clapped, waited while they got their final images, waited while everyone picked up their jackets, waited until they were out in the street and hand in hand and alone, finally, blissfully alone.

And still she waited, because she couldn't quite let this go yet. Not yet. She treasured every second that Annabel's hand was in hers. And when they got to Annabel's apartment she didn't quite know how to begin.

"What?" Annabel asked.

"I..."

"There's something wrong. I know you well enough to say that. Are you mad that I asked you and you didn't ask me?"

Indy shook her head. How to put this into words? This shattering, terrible truth that she had to tell. This thing that she didn't want to say but knew that she had to.

"I got the audition," she said. Start with the facts.

Annabel raised her eyebrows. "But that's a good thing, surely." She hesitated only a second. "Isn't it?"

Indy shook her head slowly. "No, I don't think so. Not entirely." She looked up at Annabel. "I have to stay here," she said. "And you're going to go to California."

Annabel sat. "I don't have to go."

"You don't mean that."

"Yes, yes I do."

And Indy could tell that she really did mean it. That in this moment Annabel would give up everything for her. Everything for someone that had never had a relationship last for more than a week. Everyone for someone untested, untried. And Billy had been right. She couldn't let that happen.

"But here's the thing, Annabel. I don't want you to."

She could see that the news was starting to break slowly. Annabel was sitting now and she was paler.

"The flaws," Annabel said.

Indy gave a bitter laugh. "It turns out that ignoring them only works for so long."

"We probably could have worked that out if we'd put any thought into it."

Indy nodded. She was filled with a weighty sadness. "I, um, I'm amazed with what you did. Asking me and all. I was prepared to be the one doing the asking, you know. And I know that was a big step for you."

"It was," Annabel agreed.

"And, just so you know, I like you." That didn't cover it, but if she said the other L word then she was going to cry and Annabel was going to run away like a scared rabbit. "I like you a lot, Annabel. This, us, I've adored every second of it. You're an amazing person. I don't want you to think that I don't have feelings for you."

Feelings that she couldn't admit. Feelings that she hadn't quite realized were there until she had to deny them completely. Feelings that were bigger and shinier and better than anything she'd ever had before. Feelings that were so big that she had to do this, had to let Annabel have her life, take her rewards. She had to let Annabel go. That was the top and bottom of it. If she loved her, and she did, then Annabel needed to be free to go to California without baggage, without guilt, without her.

Annabel swallowed. "Everything's catching up with us, isn't it?"

Indy nodded.

"I suppose you're right. I suppose it would be foolish for either of us to give up our dreams for a relationship that's weeks old."

Indy nodded again.

"Is it supposed to hurt this much?"

Indy's heart cracked into a million pieces at the pain in Annabel's voice. "I don't know," she said. "I've never done this before. I've never had to. Maybe we're just paying now for the happiness we had before. I'm sorry."

"You don't need to apologize for being the adult here, for forcing us both to make a sensible decision."

"That's not what I'm apologizing for. I'm apologizing because I got us into this, because I said we should ignore the flaws and go with what felt right, and if we hadn't done that, we wouldn't be sitting here right now."

"No." Annabel's eyes burned fiercely. "If we hadn't done that, we'd never have had anything. And I don't want either of us to regret what we had."

"You're right. But I'm sorry anyway. Sorry for the hurt. Sorry that life has to get in the way of us."

She stood up, unsure of what to do, unsure of whether she was allowed to touch Annabel or not. In the end, it was Annabel that stood and took her into her arms.

For a long, long time, they stood together and Indy drank in the sensation, the smell, the feel of Annabel. And there was nothing, no sound, no words, no tears. And then it had to be time. If she was doing this, she had to do it now, while she still had the strength.

She pulled herself away, walked to the door and opened it. She couldn't look back, couldn't stand to see Annabel standing alone in the middle of the living room. So she looked at the floor.

"Goodbye," she whispered gently as she closed the door behind her.

CHAPTER TWENTY EIGHT

Indy lay face down on her bed. The comforter smelled of laundry detergent and she felt better away from the light. She wished she could sleep, but she couldn't. Maybe she needed to take a pill, maybe to have a drink, but she couldn't find the energy in herself to get up and look for either of those things.

It hurt, of course it did. But more than that, there was as horrible deadness inside her, a place where it hurt so much that it didn't hurt at all. And that scared her more than she'd like to admit.

Yes, she'd done the right thing. There was no way that they could or should make this work. Annabel had been right. Risking their dreams for a relationship that had barely begun was stupid.

But it still hurt and she wanted to cry and scream and yell at the world for being stupid and unfair.

"Knock knock."

Indy sighed into the comforter. "What?"

"Checking on you," Lucinda said.

Indy rolled over. "I'm fine. Not swinging from the light fitting or hunting for razor blades."

"Okay, that's unnecessary." Lucinda slid into the room and perched on the end of Indy's bed. "How are you feeling?"

"Bereft, heartbroken, depressed, dead inside, take your pick." Lucinda sighed. "Tough, huh?"

"Tough? Yeah, you could say that." A wave of bitterness burnt her throat. "This is partially on you."

"It is?" Lucinda raised an eyebrow.

"You were the one that told me I had to start ignoring flaws, the one that said I had to stop looking for the perfect partner and settle for someone else."

"Well, was I right?" Lucinda said. "I mean, once you'd committed to more than just a first date, once you'd spent time getting to know someone for longer than a first impression, well, you did start to get feelings, didn't you?"

"Yes, but then all those flaws that you had me ignore all showed up again!"

Lucinda patted her leg. "You can be mad with me if you want, if it helps. I get that this all seems unfair to you. I get that it hurts. But—"

"No," groaned Indy. "No buts. Not now. I can't deal with learning a lesson or gaining wisdom or whatever it is that I'm supposed to have gotten out of this relationship. I'm too busy hurting and being sad."

Lucinda shrugged. "Please yourself," she said, standing up. "If you want to stew, go ahead. I guess that's you're right. But sitting here and feeling sorry for yourself isn't about to make things any better."

"And I suppose you've got the great cure-all that will fix everything?" That bitterness oozed out again.

Lucinda's eyes darkened. "I don't, Indy. I wish I did. But I do know that every relationship fails until one doesn't, that's how the world works. I do know that you can sit around feeling bad or you can try and rebuild your world a little at a time."

"What do you know about things?"

There was a small smile then. "I might not date as much as you, but that doesn't mean that I've never had my heart broken."

Indy grunted and Lucinda watched her for a moment until it was clear that the conversation was going nowhere and could only devolve into an argument. Then Lucinda walked away and Indy turned back so that her face was buried in her comforter again.

THE LAST time she'd taken Lucinda's advice was the whole reason that she was in this state in the first place. So just why she'd decided to go with her room-mate's words of wisdom again was beyond her. Indy pulled a little at her skirt, rounded her shoulders, and pushed her way through the door of the karaoke bar.

Maybe she just couldn't handle being alone again. She'd never really been alone. And now there was no Annabel to distract her she couldn't bear her own company for yet another night of staying at home.

Music throbbed around her and she tried to let it leak into her bones so that she could forget everything else.

She had to keep trying, that's what it was. She couldn't give up just because something hadn't worked out. That was the conclusion she'd finally come to. So she had to get up, dust herself off, and start all over.

From the stage a terrible rendition of *My Heart Will Go On* made her teeth hurt. She smiled a little, her first real smile in days. Okay, she could do this, back on the horse and all that. She elbowed her way over to the bar. Dutch courage first.

"What can I get you?"

The bartender was an older woman, with dancing eyes and a blue streak in her dark hair. Indy managed a semi-decent smile. "I'll take a vodka-cranberry."

"Sure thing," said the bartender, smiling right on back. "You want to see the song list?"

Indy shook her head. She came here often enough that she didn't need the list. "Just a sign-up sheet if you don't mind."

The bartender slid a sheet of paper and a battered pencil across the bar and Indy bent to scribble in her song choice. She didn't even have to think about it. A drink appeared in front of her just as she was finishing up with the form. She thanked the bartender and handed over the paper.

"Huh, nice choice," said the woman. She gave another smile and then a wink. "I'll push you to the front of the line."

And she was gone before Indy could protest. She took a breath, then a long drink. Singing would help. Being up on stage would help. It always did, it helped her forget herself, helped her disappear into something that she knew she could handle, knew she could do.

The Celine Dion enthusiast was finishing up, a raw sounding high note just slightly off key. The crowd gave him a long cheer anyway, there were points for enthusiasm around here. Indy deliberately watched the stage, keeping her eyes away from the boxes at the back, the place she'd been with Annabel.

"And up next, we've got Indy. Where are you at Indy?"

She gulped down another couple of mouthfuls before standing up and getting the attention of the host, a tall man with fake tan. Then she pushed through the crowd and jumped up on the stage.

"You ready, kid?" the host asked.

She nodded and took the mic.

The first sets of piano chords came ringing over the speakers and a spike of pain went through her heart. She hadn't even had to think about her song choice, but she hadn't *thought* about her song choice, and now it was too late.

"What would I do without your smart mouth?"

She sang, trying not to hear the words but knowing that they were eating her away even as she sang. And when she got to the chorus, when *"All of me loves all of you"* came spilling out of her mouth, it was all she could do not to burst into tears.

Somehow she did it. She finished. There was a silence before the crowd began clapping and cheering and crying out for an encore and Indy smiled as best she could and stumbled off the stage and back to the bar.

"Here, you look like you could use this."

The bartender slid a glass of amber liquid in front of her and

Indy took it gratefully, letting the burning alcohol slide down her tender throat. "Thanks."

"No worries."

She leaned on the bar, the movement revealing her cleavage as she bent, the tendrils of a tattoo curling up over her skin. Indy couldn't help but look, she was human, heart-broken not completely broken.

"You know, if you need a little help forgetting him, then I'm available," the bartender drawled.

"Forgetting her," Indy said, automatically, not moving her eyes from the bright tattoo.

"Offer still stands."

Perhaps this was what she needed. Maybe going home with the bartender would help her forget. It was worth a try, wasn't it? Perhaps if she drank enough and then... She let out a breath. "Maybe."

The bartender nodded. "Just let me know then."

The woman slid along the bar to tend to someone else and Indy was left with her drink and her thoughts, a dangerous combination.

She should do this, she'd almost decided. She had to accept that she needed to live without Annabel. It had been only a few weeks, she had no right to be so heart-broken. This had been her choice. She needed to move on.

"Hey, aren't you #IndyAnna?"

She turned to see a girl with bouncing blonde curls grinning at her. IndyAnna. It was stupid now that she thought about it. "Yeah, yeah, I guess."

"Cool," the girl said. "I loved your show. Is there gonna be a follow up? Like a moving in episode, or a real proposal or something? Because I would definitely watch that."

And all the work she'd just done persuading herself to get up and out of bed and on the stage and talking to the bartender was all undone, just like that. She gave the girl a gentle smile. This wasn't her fault, after all.

"No," she said. "No, there won't be any follow ups."

And then she reached into her pocket and pulled out a twenty, leaving it under her glass on the bar, and walked out into the night alone.

CHAPTER TWENTY NINE

"Through here you'll see our open plan office space."
Annabel peered through what looked like a porthole and saw a huge chamber filled with everything from beanbags to designer office chairs. She turned to the man next to her, who grinned.

"I know, I know. It looks a little crazy. But the ILB ethos is all about doing what it takes to give the world the best we can. That means that if you prefer working at midnight in your pajamas on a blow-up Snoopy couch, then that's what the company will give you."

"Really?" Annabel said, taking a second look at the open plan office. There was a ping pong table at one end and an array of arcade machines at the other.

"Let me guess, you're more of a formal worker?"

Annabel nodded. The guy was an intern, tasked with showing her around what could be her new company if she played her cards right. He had a shaved head and a mischievous smile and it was hard not to like him, even if she continually forgot his name. Tim. That was it. It danced in and out of her head and she kept wanting to call him Tom.

"Then we've got plenty of office space for people like you too, single offices, offices for pairs and groups, you just tell ILB what you want and how you want to work and it'll be set up for you."

"They kind of go out of their way, huh?"

Tim nodded. "Nothing is too much to ask. That's part of the reason that there's such a high demand to work here, and definitely the reason that we're so selective about who we invite to collaborate with us."

They began to walk down a long corridor lined with magazine articles and newspaper cut-outs of everything from the moon landing to the first iPhone release.

"So, what are you looking to bring to the table?" Tim asked.

Annabel raised an eyebrow at him and he laughed.

"Sorry, it takes a little getting used to," he said. "We're fully open about all projects that we work on here, there's no secrets. The idea is that we have all the greatest minds in tech right here and we should allow input from everyone to produce the best… whatever it is that we're producing at the moment. And that runs the gamut from a medical app designed to regulate blood sugar in diabetics to a team working on fuel that will be more efficient for space flight."

"Math," Annabel said. "That's what I'm here for. Algorithms specifically." She wasn't about to give too much away, no contracts had been signed yet.

"Cool," Tim said. "I've been playing around with a little something on the side, looking to improve search results in scientific journals. Maybe you could drop by my desk and take a look at it?"

She'd been immersed, she realized. Immersed so far in what she was seeing and hearing that she'd almost forgotten. For a second there her heart had been beating like normal and she could breathe without pain.

But Tim's hopeful smile had shattered that illusion and she was hit again by the fact that she was alone. Without Indy.

Which, of course, was exactly as it should be, as she told herself every morning when she woke up. She was supposed to be alone. Not something that she felt like explaining to the hopeful looking man at her side though. The curve of his smile, the slight leaning in told her that he was hoping for more than career advice.

"I, uh, I'm gay," she offered.

There was something that she'd never had a problem saying, a label that had fit her since the first time she'd tried it on. He grinned wider and leaned back again, shrugging. "That's cool. I'd welcome your input anyway, and maybe even a welcome beer when you get settled here? It's not terribly hard making friends here, we're a nice bunch, but it helps to know someone coming in."

She found herself smiling back. He was a nice guy, and he was right. Not that she needed friends either, but, well, it'd be nice to have someone to bounce ideas off now that she and Billy were... whatever they were.

Divorced was kind of the way it seemed.

Divorced from her business partner and split from the only woman she'd ever let into her life.

Way to go.

She swallowed and hurried along, following Tim onto the next part of their tour.

CALIFORNIA WAS stereotypically sunny. Palm trees reached up to endless blue skies and Annabel shrugged off her blazer and let the sun sting her bare arms.

A little north of Palo Alto, a place she'd dreamed after, longed after, a place she could call home, a place she could be successful, a place where she could surround herself with the best and the brightest minds in the business.

Exactly what she'd always wanted.

The cafe was neat and small with tables spilling out on the sidewalk and people chattering. A young couple walked past, hand in hand and Annabel's stomach flipped.

She didn't want that.

She didn't want a person, she didn't want to be tied down, she wanted to be alone. She was better alone. She wanted to concentrate on her work. She wanted to be right here, where she was, in

Silicon Valley.

But, said a little voice in the back of her head, if she didn't want that, then why did it hurt to see the couple go by? If she didn't want that, then why could she still feel Indy's hand in her own? If she didn't want that, then why was she so reluctant to go back to her empty hotel room?

This had to be. It was right. She just had to work on remembering that more of the time. And possibly she needed to avoid coffee shops. The couple at the next table exchanged a noisy smooch and she slid her sunglasses on and turned away.

Life without Indy. She could definitely do it. She'd done it before, after all. So why was it so hard now? Why was it so difficult to close her eyes and not see Indy's sharp features, her turquoise eyes, her curves and her freckles and her flowing hair?

Jesus Christ. All she'd ever wanted was right here on a plate in front of her and she had to spoil it all by getting emotional over a woman.

Her phone rang.

"So? How is it?" Billy's voice sounded far away. Well, he was far away.

"It's fantastic, amazing, just what I've always wanted." Even to herself her voice sounded empty.

"Great, I'm so happy for you, Annabel. You deserve all this."

She covered up a sigh. "Thanks. You calling just to check up on me?"

She could hear Cassie's voice in the background urging Billy to say something.

"Tell her?" Billy said, muffled, obviously talking to Cassie.

"Of course," Cassie's voice said.

"But I thought—"

"Not that," interrupted Cassie. "The other."

"Oh, Jesus, yes, of course." Billy's voice got clearer again and Annabel wondered what exactly was going on back in the city. "So, I've got news."

"News?"

"We did it."

"Did what?" Billy wasn't helping with her confusion.

"We did it," he said again. "We're rich. We sold a company. We did what we always said we'd do. Agreements are all made, the lawyers are all happy, the only things missing are our signatures on the final documents. After that, we're free."

Was it just her? Or did Billy sound a little less ecstatic than she'd expected?

"That's amazing," she said, injecting as much enthusiasm into her voice as she could and knowing that she was falling short, that they were both falling short.

"Listen, I've set up an appointment to get all the necessary signatures for when you get back," Billy said. "And I thought that maybe after that you and I could go to dinner. Just us. A celebration and all."

She smiled a little as the sunshine stroked her face. "Yes. I'd like that."

She should be happy, she thought as she put the phone down again. She really should. Everything she'd ever wanted. It was all there, all happening now.

So why didn't she feel happier? Fuller? Better?

And, now that she was thinking about it, what exactly had Billy and Cassie been talking about in hushed whispers? There were obviously two pieces of news, one thing she was supposed to know, and one she wasn't. But what could be so important that Billy would rank it on the same level as selling LBN?

The couple at the next table were feeding each other cheesecake and Annabel shook her head. She couldn't watch this.

She drained her coffee and stood up, picking up her blazer in one hand. Back to the hotel it was. One more night here and then she'd be signing her new contract in the morning. Then back to the city to pack up her life and move.

Just what she'd always wanted.

Except... Except a little tiny part of her didn't want this anymore. No, that wasn't quite true. A little tiny part of her wanted this but also something else.

A little tiny part of her wanted Indy to hold her hand.

CHAPTER THIRTY

Her fingers found their places on the strings and she closed her eyes, letting the words wash over her and disappearing into the music. This she could do. This was the only thing she could do. She had to make this work.

"Stop, stop, stop."

The voice came over her headphones and the backing track stopped playing and she let her hands drop. She tried to smile, tried to keep a positive attitude, but this was the fourth time in as many minutes that Bethany had stopped her.

"Yes?" she asked, trying to stay polite.

There was a short pause, then the door opened and Bethany herself came into the tiny studio. She had a half-shaved head and an eyebrow ring and a tattoo was peeking out from the neck of her t-shirt. But she knew her stuff, Indy could tell.

"Are you feeling okay?" the producer asked.

"Sure," shrugged Indy.

"A little nervous, maybe?"

Indy shook her head. "Not really. I mean, singing into a mic in a closed room is kind of easier than doing it in front of people. Microphones generally don't boo or throw things."

Bethany grinned. "Right. Do you need anything? Some more water maybe? Or a snack? Or, well, maybe something a little, um, a little more rock and roll?"

Indy shook her head. "No, really, I'm totally fine."

Bethany shifted her weight from one foot to another. "Okay. That's good. It's just, well, um, this isn't quite what we're going for."

"What isn't?" Indy asked, confused. "This is the song that I was told to play, I'm sure of it, unless there's been some mistake?"

"No, it's not that. The song's fine," Bethany said. "It's just, well, we're looking for something more upbeat, you know?"

"Upbeat?"

"Yeah, think a little more Katie Perry-ish."

"Katy Perry-ish."

"Right."

"And, um, what am I doing wrong?"

Bethany scratched her nose. "You're giving us a lot of Elliott Smith," she said with a wry smile. "The song is great, it's just, we need more of your energy, the kind of energy you had on the demo track. Maybe go a little faster, inject a little oomph into your voice, smile more."

"Smile more." She hadn't known that she wasn't smiling.

"This isn't supposed to be a test. We already love you, and love your song. So chill out a little, have some more fun with it. Can you do that?"

Jesus. Maybe she should have accepted the offer of 'something a little more rock and roll.' Maybe a drink would help take the edge off. But she nodded anyway.

Bethany grinned again and went back out and Indy pulled her headphones back on.

"Whenever you're ready," Bethany said from the sound booth.

Indy took a breath. She could do this. She had to do this. She closed her eyes again, summoning up visions of things that made her happy, feeling a new energy flowing through her veins. Ice cream on a hot day, an iced Coke, Annabel taking her hand for the first time.

She held the picture in her head as she started to play, speeding the song up just a touch, singing it to Annabel. To that Annabel, the one that took her hand, the one she had been when they'd been ignoring their flaws, the one she'd borrowed for a little while.

"Great, perfect," Bethany said, once the final chord had died away. "Exactly what we needed. Well done."

But Indy's eyes were still closed. She was reluctant to let go of the image of Annabel that she had in her head.

SHE WENT straight into the kitchen, dumping her bag next to the door, standing her guitar up against the counter, and dropping her keys on the table.

"So, how did it go?"

"Good," she said. "Good. Great. It was… harder than I thought maybe. But the first track is done."

Lucinda grinned. "Is a celebration in order then?"

Indy sat down, more tired than she could ever remember being before. "I don't know. Not tonight maybe, eh?"

Lucinda sighed and closed her book, a hugely heavy tome with a name so long that Indy couldn't read it from the other side of the table. "How are you feeling then?"

Indy shrugged. "How am I supposed to feel? Tired. Sad. Exhausted. Bereft. Does this shit actually get any better?"

Lucinda got up and took a bottle of wine from the counter and found two glasses in the cupboard. She pulled a corkscrew from the drawer and began drilling it into the cork. "Yes. Usually. I mean, if it didn't, people would just walk around depressed all the time, wouldn't they?"

Wine glugged into glasses and Indy accepted the drink when it was passed to her. "I suppose so," she said.

Lucinda sat down again. "Usually you bounce right back," she said. "What's so different this time? Why does this one hurt so much more?"

"Because it was different," said Indy. "Because… Because maybe Annabel was The One. And maybe I let her go because I had to. And maybe there won't be another one."

"You're such a romantic," Lucinda said. "You can't possibly believe that there's only one person for every other person. That's crazy."

"Maybe it is," said Indy. "I don't know anymore."

"No," Lucinda said. "You know what, that's wrong. You're wrong. Romance is a decision. Falling in love is a decision. And the reason that this time was different was because you actually allowed yourself to do it. You stuck around long enough that you got real feelings."

Indy was too tired to get mad or defensive. Besides, probably Lucinda was right. "Fine. But in that case, I've made my decision, haven't I? I did what I had to do."

"Decisions can be unmade," said Lucinda.

"No. Not this one. It wouldn't be fair."

"So now you get to decide what's fair?"

"Annabel had her life planned out. She knows what she wants. And I've got no right to disrupt that. She thought she wanted to be alone and discovered that she didn't, which is great for her. But that doesn't necessarily mean she needs to be with me. She needs to follow her goals first, she's worked hard for what she's achieved. I made the right decision."

"And what about your goals?" Lucinda cradled her glass in her hands.

"My stupid bucket list? Is that a goal?"

"It's a list of goals." Lucinda leaned forward. "You know what the problem is with your bucket list?"

"It's dumb."

"No. It's too positive. You only put the good things on the list. Sometimes life needs bad things too, so that you can appreciate the good, you know?"

"Are you suggesting that I add 'get heart broken' to my bucket list?"

"Well, at least you'd be able to cross something off," said Lucinda. "What do you want?"

Indy laughed, but it wasn't a real laugh. "I want everything. I want to record my songs, I want Annabel to have her dream job, and I want the two of us to be together. But that's unrealistic."

"Is it though?"

Indy rolled her eyes. "You know, you're not actually making this any easier. I've made my decision, that's it. End of story. I did what was best."

"What would it take to convince you that you were wrong?"

Indy laughed that sad laugh again and shook her head. "Nothing. Everything."

"Annabel crawling on her knees to beg you to take her back?"

"I guess that would do it."

"So there is a chance," said Lucinda, topping up her wine.

"No. Annabel would never do that. She was sad, sure. But the second she gets out to California she'll know that this was all for the best. She'll have everything she's ever wanted."

"And you don't fit into that picture?"

Indy drank deeply from her glass, emptying half of it in one go before pushing it back down the table to Lucinda. "I don't fit into that picture. Which means I did the right thing. Which means I need to get over myself and move on."

Which was easier said than done because every time she closed her eyes she thought about Annabel.

"Whatever you say," Lucinda said, filling up Indy's glass again. "But you don't have to play by the rules, you know?"

Indy took her glass back. "What rules?"

Lucinda grinned. "I'm just saying that sometimes life is better when you make up your own rules as you go along."

"Helpful, Luce. Thanks."

"Don't mention it. I'm the old wise woman, remember?"

"Old, wise, and getting drunk by the sounds of it," Indy replied.

"In vino veritas and all that," Lucinda said. "Things'll turn out for the best, just you wait and see."

Which was very, very hard to believe. But Indy smiled anyway. Lucinda was trying to help. Not that she thought anyone could help her now. Now she just had to live with the decision she'd made, it was really that simple.

CHAPTER THIRTY ONE

Signing her name on the dotted line felt like ending a whole section of her life. It was ending a section of her life, she assumed. And as the others in the room cheered and laughed she found that it made her face ache to force a smile onto it.

"Let's get out of here," Billy said in her ear.

His curls were gelled down and in his smart suit he looked every inch the successful businessman. When all this had started he'd been a guy with an afro in ripped jeans and a Metallica t-shirt. How far they'd come.

"So, how does it feel to be rich?" Billy asked as they stepped into the elevator.

"I could ask you the same thing."

"Weird, isn't it?"

"Maybe the reality of it all hasn't set in yet," Annabel said, doubtfully.

"Or maybe this isn't what we planned at all," said Billy. He sounded sad and she wrapped her arm around his. "Or maybe it is," he added. "And I just haven't realized yet that I can technically buy Rhode Island."

"I don't think they let you do that, purchase states individually. I think it's like a six-pack, all or nothing."

"Huh," said Billy. "I guess I'll have to start saving up then."

When they stepped out of the building he hailed a cab and they both crawled into it.

"So, this is finally it then," Billy said, settling back.

Annabel studied him. "Are we still going to be friends?"

He sat straight upright again in alarm. "Is that what you've been worried about this whole time? Jesus, Annabel."

"No, not exactly, well, a little, I guess."

Billy took her hand. "Of course we'll still be friends. Although I guess we'll see each other a little less often. I couldn't have done this without you, Annabel. I don't think either of us could have done this alone. You were the best man at my wedding, how could you think that we wouldn't be friends anymore?"

Annabel grinned and felt a little lighter. "I'm just waiting for that invitation to become a godmother," she said, crossing her legs.

A shadow passed over Billy's face and he stared out of the window for a second. Then he pulled himself back to the conversation. "So what has been bothering you then?" he asked. "If it wasn't you and I not being friends, was it just the shock of suddenly becoming rich and selling everything we've ever worked for?"

"A bit," she said, wondering just how much to tell him. As much as she adored him, there were some things that it was just easier to talk to Cassie about.

"Is it Indy?"

Crap. She forgot that Billy could be psychic when he needed to be. She nodded, miserably.

"It didn't work out then?"

"How could it? She has work here in the city. I'm moving to the other side of the country. We'd been together for all of a few weeks, risking our careers for something that new, that young would be ridiculous." It sounded good and solid when she said it, not like an excuse, more of a justification.

Billy snorted. "Right."

"And what exactly is that supposed to mean?"

Billy was rescued from answering by the cab drawing up at the curb.

Annabel looked out of the window, then back at Billy. "Seriously? The Olive Garden?"

"Well, I thought about somewhere fancier, but it didn't really seem like us," Billy said as he peeled off a bill to pay the driver. "Besides, endless breadsticks."

Annabel laughed as she got out of the cab. Billy was right. This was a whole lot more them. She was still smiling as they were guided to a table.

"I wish you were happier," Billy said, once they'd ordered.

"I could say the same about you."

Billy ignored the comment. "Do you love her?"

"What?"

"It's a simple question. Do you love Indy?"

Cutlery clinked and the hum of voices was like background music. Finally, inexorably, Annabel nodded.

"Then why did you let her go?"

"I told you why."

"You told me about a bunch of logistics," Billy said, snapping a breadstick in half. "Or is that all just your excuse? Because you'd rather be alone, because being alone is better, easier, you don't have to work at it?"

Annabel felt stung. "No!"

"Really?"

She took a breath. "Okay, three months ago, yes, you'd have been right. But not now. Things have changed, I've changed. I see it now. I see why your eyes light up when you see Cassie. I see why people don't spend their lives alone. I honestly do. But this, this couldn't work out, Billy. You have to trust me on that."

Plates came but Billy didn't touch his. She could tell that he was working his way up to something and she didn't know what it was. She took a bite of pasta, waiting for him to find the courage or the strength to say what he was going to say.

When it finally blurted out, it took her a full half a minute to understand what he'd actually said.

"I'm probably infertile."

She slowly put her fork down, lifting her eyes to his and he was flushed.

"I know that you and I don't normally talk about stuff like this," he said. "But you should know this. The reason that I haven't been in the office much is that we've been going to a bunch of doctors and, well, the results are in and it looks like I'm shooting blanks."

He took a large gulp from his glass of water and Annabel sat there aghast. She didn't know what to say. For as long as she could remember Billy had wanted children. Even before he met Cassie his plan had always been to get rich and raise an army of kids on a yacht somewhere.

"Billy, I..." She took another deep breath and let the honesty out. "I'm so sorry, Billy. I know how much this means to you."

He shrugged, picking up his fork. "I'm getting used to the idea, slowly," he said. "There's a few things we can try. If they don't work, then we'll start looking into adoption as well. I just—"

He reached again for the water and even if she hadn't just heard his voice nearly break she'd know that he was close to tears. He swallowed and blinked and she reached for his hand.

"I feel broken," he said, looking at the table.

She saw destruction on his face and her heart went out to him. "I'm so sorry. I wish there was something I could do."

He twisted himself into a smile. "I'll get through this. Cass and I will get through this. It's just been a little rough, that's all."

"Obviously."

He took a mouthful of his chicken and chewed it slowly as though he was thinking and Annabel couldn't help but think how bad a friend she must have been not to notice that something so terrible was happening.

And she'd talked to Cassie, poured out her problems, and Cassie had listened as though she had no worries of her own.

"There is something you can do, Annabel."

She raised her eyes to his in confusion. "There is?"

"Be happy."

She laughed a little, unsure of what he meant.

"I mean it, Annabel. There's a huge chance here that I'm not going to have what I want. And there's you sitting there with what you want inches from your fingertips and the reason that you're not taking it is that you're scared."

"No, I told you—"

"What you told me was bullshit, an excuse. You're afraid of trying and failing, you're afraid of breaking yourself if you push this too far and you don't succeed, but you know what? That's life. The only things worth having are the ones that it would kill you not to have. You're being a fool, Annabel. And that's not like you."

She opened her mouth to speak, then closed it again. Only after a second had passed did she open it once more. "What if she says no?"

Not the question she'd expected to ask, but there it was.

"She might," said Billy. "If the two of you have already agreed to move on, if she's already agreed to move on, maybe she will. But she might not. And you won't know unless you ask her, will you?"

Ask her. Could it really be that simple?

Annabel's heart started to beat faster. She'd written all this off, she'd deliberately denied herself happiness, she'd assumed she still wanted the same things as she'd wanted a decade ago. But now she wasn't so sure.

"Annabel, you love the woman. You'd be an idiot to let her go just because you're too stubborn or ashamed to ask for a second chance."

And she'd never heard anything so true in her life.

CHAPTER THIRTY TWO

It had been Indy that had called things off. She'd just gone along with it, swayed by the sense of it all, and, yes, Billy had been right, out of pure fear. Fear that things weren't going to work out, fear that things would work out.

In the back of Annabel's head it had been easier to agree to split. That way she had control. But, and here was the thing, she'd always had control. She had control now, if what she wanted was Indy back.

She took deep breaths, drinking in the scent of coffee, trying to center herself and her mind. But it was useless. She already knew the answer. She'd known from the second Indy had closed the door behind her. Indy was something, someone special. Her world was a better place with Indy in it. The disruption she'd thought another person would bring to her life was nothing more than her fear talking.

What Indy really did was make her whole life brighter.

And she wanted that back.

However they'd have to make it work, whatever she'd have to do or sacrifice, she wanted Indy back in her life.

"Annabel?"

She opened her eyes and saw Laura staring at her in bemusement. "Oh, hi, uh, yes, won't you sit down?" That sounded way too formal.

"Let me grab a coffee first," Laura said, good-naturedly. "Want anything?"

"No, I'm fine."

She waited while Laura got her drink, still not sure of exactly how to do this thing but knowing that she needed help. Also knowing that she was going to have to open up to someone, namely Laura. Never an easy thing for her to do.

"So, what's up?" Laura asked. "Congrats on the sale, by the way."

"Thanks," Annabel said. "Um, okay, this is weird. I, uh, I don't really know how to say this."

Laura's eyes crinkled into a smile. She leaned in and her voice was softer when she spoke. "Annabel, you're not my boss anymore. I get that. But, well, there is something that you should know."

"Okay," Annabel said slowly.

"Lars and I are engaged. We're getting married in a month."

Annabel frowned, trying to puzzle out the connection here and failing. "Um, that's nice?" she offered, finally.

Laura's eyes widened. "Oh, I thought… Never mind. No, I just thought…"

And it dawned on Annabel. "You thought I was hitting on you and going to ask you out."

Laura blushed. "It had crossed my mind."

Just like that, the ice was broken. Annabel laughed. "No. Not that you're not attractive, you are, but that's the exact opposite of what I want your help with."

"So… You want to break up with me?" Laura joked.

Annabel grinned again. "Not quite. I need your help getting Indy back."

Laura's mouth turned into a little round O and Annabel laughed again before finally explaining herself.

"So, you want to get back together?" Laura said, finally.

"Yes," Annabel said with utter confidence and decision. "But, well, I'm not always great at personal relations and I'm not sure I can do what I need to do face to face. Does that sound cowardly?"

"No, it's kind of sweet."

"I just... I want this to be right and I'm afraid that I'll stumble and mess things up if I do it live. That and considering the way we met, what we've done together, it seems kind of... apt," Annabel went on.

"So you want to record a video."

"Something short, something I can send to her over social media or email."

The idea had come to her in the night when she'd been sweating and worrying over how she was going to do this, what she was going to say. And it seemed like the perfect solution. They were social media's golden couple, so what better way to open her heart than on video?

"Alright," Laura said, grinning now. "Let's do it. It's a brilliant idea."

Annabel slumped in relief. She needed Laura's help to do this properly and had been crossing her fingers that the woman would agree. She picked up her glass of water, more relaxed now. "So, you and Lars?"

Laura rolled her eyes. "If you're about to tell me that you thought we were related, we're not, I swear."

"No," Annabel said, though she'd been about to do exactly that. "I was going to ask you if you're happy."

Laura smiled. "I feel... like I've found what was missing in my life."

And that, Annabel thought, summed up how she felt about Indy perfectly. Except she hadn't known that there'd been something missing in the first place.

LAURA CLOSED the door behind her, leaving Annabel alone with the camera. It was all set up, all she had to do was press the button on the remote in her hand.

She was nervous now, more nervous than she'd thought she'd be. And she had no plan. Not one word scripted. This had to be done right and the only way to do that was to speak from the heart.

Her heart beat hard and her hands were sweating and she closed her eyes for one more second. It was fine. She could do this. Only Indy was going to see it, and if she couldn't open her heart to Indy, then what hope did they have?

She opened her eyes.

She pressed the button.

"I always thought love was for other people. I was always happy alone, happier with numbers and with code than talking face to face. The day that I cracked the algorithm for Love By Numbers was the best day of my life."

She smiled, remembering the day.

"Then you walked into my life and destroyed everything. My perfect algorithm was flawed, it had matched me with someone I could never be interested in, simply because I could never be interested in anyone. I was better off alone."

Okay, maybe this was going as well as she hoped. Maybe Laura could erase it and start over? She took a breath. She might as well finish, say what she needed to say, get it all out there.

"The truth of the matter is, that the algorithm, my algorithm, was better than even I had expected. Because I fell in love with you. No matter how different we are, no matter what I wanted or didn't want, I fell absolutely and completely in love with you."

"For the first time I wanted to share something with someone. I wanted to share my life. I wanted to wake up next to someone. I wanted to be with you."

"I once told Billy that I was in the romance business for money. I thought that was true. I'm not exactly the most romantic of people, in case you hadn't noticed. But I'm going to try my hardest here, even though I've never done this before."

Another deep breath.

"Indy, you make my world turn, you make the sun shine brighter, you make me want to smile every second of every day, you are beautiful and brilliant and I love you. Just knowing that you exist is enough to make me a happier person."

"And I know there are flaws in our relationship, I know there are problems and differences and things that seem hard. But, here's the thing, I'm starting to think that those might be the things that make this relationship worth having. That having to work for something makes it so much more precious."

The final stretch. Annabel took the deepest of breaths.

"Indy, please come back to me. I love you. We can do anything together. I want to make this work, no matter what sacrifices need to be made. Because you, we, are worth all the sacrifices in the world."

"WOW," LAURA said, minimizing the video.

"You didn't edit anything?" asked Annabel, feeling slightly sick at the sound of her own voice and the sight of her own face on the screen.

"No," Laura said. "It's perfect the way it is. It's you. It's everything you wanted to say and more."

"You're sure?"

"Dead sure."

"So all I have to do is send it," Annabel said, her knees feeling weak.

Laura scraped back her chair and pulled Annabel toward it. "Sit down and send it now. If you don't, you'll spend weeks agonizing over it. It's like ripping off a band-aid. I'm going to grab a soda."

Annabel sat down. Laura was right. She had to send the damn video. She bought it up again, hit the share link. Was she really going to do this?

She was terrified and excited all at the same time. She closed her eyes tight shut and hit the mouse button and heard the whooshing sound of the file being sent.

She still had her eyes closed, pulse slowly coming back to normal, when Laura came back.

"Did you send it?" Laura asked, popping open a can of soda. "Well done, you—" She stopped dead in the middle of her sentence.

"What?" Annabel asked. "What?"

Laura's face was pale. "Um, you sent the video," she said. "That's the good news. But there's some bad news too."

Annabel's stomach sank.

"You just posted the entire thing to the #IndyAnna Twitter account."

CHAPTER THIRTY THREE

Indy felt her phone buzz in her pocket as she was leaving the studio. She pulled it out for long enough to check the notification then had to scramble for her bus. Only once on the bus did she get her phone out again.

"Trouble in paradise?" said the message. She checked the sender. Evelyn. And there was a link. She frowned. It was probably nothing, a mistake, Evelyn hadn't exactly sent her a ton of messages before. Maybe it was spam or some kind of scam. She wasn't about to hit that link just on the off-chance.

It had been a day. Playing made her happy, it honestly did. Yet an entire day playing at the studio had left her feeling less exuberant than she'd expected. A month ago, sitting at her desk in the call center, she'd dreamed of a life like this. But... But it was exhausting and now she was worried that turning music into her job would mean losing out on some of the joy of it.

She was glad to get home, propping her guitar case up by the door. She was shedding her coat and trying to decide whether to eat or shower first when Lucinda appeared.

"Have you seen it?"

"Seen what?" Indy asked, tiredly.

"Of course you haven't. You couldn't have. Or else you'd be... I don't know. Either super depressed and angry or ecstatic, I can't tell. Here, come on, come into the kitchen, you can watch it on my phone."

Indy tried to follow the conversation as best she could. "Watch something that's going to make me either depressed or ecstatic?" she said.

"Yes, come on."

She shook her head. "No, those odds are too low for me. I've had a hell of a day, I'm going to take a shower."

"Jesus," Lucinda puffed. "Sometimes, I just can't believe how out of touch you are with the world. This is important, Indy. You need to see this. Trust me. Please. Just trust me."

With a roll of her eyes, Indy finally followed Lucinda into the kitchen. Lucinda was like a dog with a bone when she got an idea into her head and sometimes it was better to just humor her. The faster she watched this damn whatever-it-was the faster she could get a hot shower and some comforting mac and cheese.

"What?" she said, letting herself be sat down on a kitchen chair.

"Just quiet. Watch."

Lucinda toggled her screen on and balanced her phone against a cup on the table. A video was buffering and an instant later Annabel's face appeared. The shock of it took her breath away. She'd been trying to forget, and yet she'd forgotten nothing, not the angle of her cheekbones, not the shade of her eyes, not a thing.

"I always thought love was for other people," Annabel began.

Indy was barely listening, could barely process what was happening. But as Annabel spoke she leaned in closer and closer, her ears finally tuning in to what was being said, to the meaning and the emotion behind the words.

When the video finally finished, tears were pouring down her face.

"What—" started Lucinda.

Indy waved her off, and set the video back to the beginning, running it over again and again, wanting to believe every word but afraid that she couldn't, that she didn't dare.

Only after the third time did she let the phone screen go dark again.

"This is everywhere," Lucinda said. "All over the internet. If you think you guys were trending before, well, this is going nuts."

Indy couldn't believe it. "Show me."

Lucinda did. She scrolled through Twitter, Reddit, Facebook, every possible social media site. #IndyAnna was trending everywhere. This, Indy finally realized, was what Evelyn's message had been about.

"It's really everywhere," she said.

Lucinda laid a hand on her arm. "It is. But you're going to be okay, I know this is an invasion of your privacy but—"

"No," Indy said. "You don't understand. I'm not mad."

How could she be mad? Annabel, private, personal, closed off Annabel had put her heart on the line, and she'd done it in front of millions of people. This had to be real.

"You're not?" Lucinda asked.

Indy shook her head. "I'm... impressed."

Lucinda pulled out a chair and sat down. "Indy, this is... weird."

"Is it really though?" Indy asked. "We met online, technically. Our whole relationship was based on a computer algorithm. Everything we've done has been played out on the internet. Is it so weird that Annabel would choose this as a way to get to me?"

"Why not just, I don't know, come and knock on the door?" Lucinda asked.

Indy grinned. "Because she's Annabel and she's not always great at talking to other people and because she needed to make a romantic gesture, and, well, for Annabel this is a romantic gesture."

Lucinda peered at her closely. "And what about for you? Is this a romantic gesture for you?"

"Yes." The answer was simple. This was so perfectly messed up and weird that it was exactly what she'd needed.

Lucinda crossed her arms. "Can I be the adult for a second

here?"

"Do you have to be?"

"Yes. One of us does. Indy, you need to decide what you want. You need to decide what you're going to risk and how. You need to know your own heart, because if you don't, you're going to break someone else's."

Indy nodded. Lucinda was right.

"Do you love her?"

Did she? What kind of question was that? It was like she'd never felt anything before. Like she'd been waiting her whole life for this moment. Like she couldn't imagine her life going any other way.

"I love her with all my heart."

"And what about your careers and the distance and all the other flaws?"

"We'll learn to deal with them," Indy said. "Because that's what love is, isn't it? It's learning how to compromise, learn how to love in spite of something, balancing things out." She reached out to take Lucinda's hand. "Luce, I need this. I want this. I can't think of any other thing that I've ever wanted like this. I made the wrong decision. I think I've known that for a while now, deep down, and I'm getting the chance to make that decision again. This is why everything in my life has felt so wrong, so different. Because I'm on a path I'm not supposed to be on."

"You're not just checking off a box on your bucket list?"

Indy shook her head. "I swear I'm not. I swear I need this."

"Then what are you waiting for!" Lucinda said. "Find the woman and tell her you love her back. Fast, before she changes her mind!"

SHE DID everything she could think of. Direct messages on every platform she had an account with, calling Annabel's phone until it rang out and then calling and calling it again. She called LBN, only to be told that Annabel was no longer working there. And nothing. Nothing. An hour since she'd seen the video and she was going mad with the fact that she simply couldn't track Annabel down.

In the end, she called the only number she had for anyone other than Annabel at LBN.

"Laura speaking."

"Laura, it's Indy."

"Indy, I—"

"No time," Indy gabbled. "I need to know what's the name of the company that Annabel's going to work for in California?"

"Uh, ILB Think Tank," Laura said. "But Indy, I—"

"Thanks," interrupted Indy, hanging up.

ILB Think Tank. She googled it quickly. Based in Palo Alto, California. Okay. That was far, but okay.

She had to do something. She'd start tearing the walls down if she didn't act. And this was better done in person, wasn't it? That way they could fall into each other's arms. That way she could see Annabel's smile, taste her again. That way they could be together all the sooner. And she didn't care if she never came back. She didn't care if she never set foot in a studio ever again. Because, she was realizing, this, her and Annabel, it mattered more than anything else. Anything.

"What are you doing?" Lucinda asked, coming into the kitchen to find Indy with her laptop open.

"Going to reclaim my girlfriend," Indy said, skin prickling at the word girlfriend. Girlfriend. She could get used to that.

"Okay," said Lucinda slowly. "But what are you exactly actually doing right now."

Indy looked up at her and grinned. "Buying a plane ticket to California."

For a brief moment she thought that Lucinda might play the grown-up card again, that she might try to stop her. But then Lucinda spoke. "Need cash for that? Or do you have it covered?"

"I'm putting it on my credit card," said Indy. "And, um, thanks for not stopping me."

Lucinda grinned back. "Only the oldest and wisest women know when to back off. There's no getting in the way of true

love."
 True love.
 Indy's heart rate tripled.
 True love.

CHAPTER THIRTY FOUR

What was done, was done, was the way she'd chosen to look at it. And as Laura pointed out, scrubbing the video from the Twitter feed was likely to look even worse than leaving the thing there. At least this way she was owning her actions.

Which had two knock-on effects.

The first was that LBN were likely to be unimpressed that she'd inadvertently revealed that the web series was faked. Not so much of a problem when you owned the company, more of one when you didn't.

The second was that she had no idea how Indy would feel about her splashing their private life all over the internet. To be fair, their private life had already been splashed all over the internet. But still, this was something she should have done privately. It was something, she now realized, that she really should have done in person.

It took all of an hour before she couldn't take it anymore. The constant buzzing and beeping of notifications, the shaking hands every time she picked up her phone. So she muted the alerts and went running, the only thing that was likely to calm her head.

A run, a shower, and a nap, and then she'd deal with the chaos that she'd created, that was the plan. Right up until she opened a sticky eye to a strangely pale looking light and realized that she'd slept through most of the night.

Annabel banged her head back onto the pillow and groaned. What had she done? Spilling her heart out over the internet to anyone and everyone. The new owners of LBN had every right to be angry, and potentially to start legal action. And Indy... Indy had every right to want to punch her. Or never see her again. She groaned again.

It was a half hour and a shower before she could face her phone. As she poured orange juice she pressed her finger onto the print sensor, only to find that it wasn't working. She growled and her glass nearly overflowed and then, horrified, she realized that she'd screwed up yet again. Rather than silencing her Twitter notifications, she'd turned her whole damn phone off.

The wait while the phone re-booted was agonizing. And then the notifications started coming in. Tons of Twitter and Facebook icons, a text from Billy asking what the hell she'd done, a text from Laura asking if she was doing okay, and... seven missed calls.

All from Indy.

Jesus.

There were no more thoughts of breakfast. She put the juice carton away and stared at her phone. There was no voicemail icon. Which meant that she'd need to call Indy back. Call back the woman to whom she'd declared undying love in front of literally the entire world and then switched off her phone to become uncontactable. Brilliant.

But this was her own doing. She had chosen this. She wanted this, she wanted to get Indy's attention and there was no denying the fact that this was an attention-grabbing move. She had to face the consequences of her actions.

Hands trembling, she called back.

Nothing.

Just a sugary voice telling her that the number was unavailable.

Annabel slumped back in her seat.

Had she screwed up so badly that Indy had even changed her number?

Her heart was thudding in her chest and she almost, almost gave up. She wanted to crawl into her bed and stick her head under the covers. But she wouldn't. This was worth fighting for, she reminded herself. This was what she wanted and she was damned if she wasn't going to go down kicking and punching. She called another number.

"Laura."

"Jeez, Annabel, it's like seven in the morning."

"Seven forty-five," said Annabel. "And I need to know Indy's address."

There was silence on the phone. Then: "Are you okay?"

"I'm fine, but I need the address, it's important."

"I can't access LBN personnel files, Annabel, it's unethical and…" There was a flurry of something on the other end of the phone. Then Laura came back. "Okay, okay. Lars knows the address without looking it up. It's across the street from his brother's place, so he remembers it. Got a pen?"

Annabel bit the cap off a pen and scribbled down the address she was given.

"Thanks. Are you going into work today?"

"Yes," said Laura. "And before you ask, I'll keep an ear out for any news. I can't imagine that the new bosses will be thrilled, but maybe there's a way to spin this to make you look better."

"You're a life-saver," Annabel said and hung up in a hurry now.

THE NAME was on the bell, which was fortunate since she had no apartment number. But the voice that came over the intercom wasn't familiar.

"I, um, I'm looking for Indy?"

A crackling noise. "She's not here."

Crap. "Could you tell me where she is? This is Annabel."

A long pause. "You'd better come up." The buzzer buzzed and

the door clicked open.

A tall woman was waiting in an open door. She looked strict, strong, slightly foreboding. But then she smiled and suddenly the hallway was bathed in light.

"Annabel? I'm Lucinda, Indy's room-mate, it's nice to meet you at last. Can I get you something?" She walked into the apartment and Annabel followed. "A coffee maybe? Or pastries, I just stopped by at the bakery on my way back from morning yoga in the park. Help yourself, they're on the table."

They were in a pleasant kitchen, surfaces muddled with condiments and spices, letters and stickers pinned to the refrigerator. The smell of coffee was strong and Annabel's mouth watered. "I wouldn't mind a coffee."

Lucinda grabbed a mug and poured. "I'm serious about the pastries. Take one at least. I think I forgot that Indy wasn't here, or maybe my eyes are just bigger than my stomach. I can't eat all those."

A towering pile of croissants and other delights was on the table and Annabel took a danish, her stomach rumbling. She took a bite before hastily swallowing it, remembering what she was supposed to be doing. "Can you tell me where Indy is?" she asked. "It's important that I find her."

"I should say so," said Lucinda, sitting down. "I've seen the video."

Annabel groaned. "The whole world has seen the video."

Lucinda shrugged. "That's what you get for playing around with social media. Accidents will happen." She took a mouthful of coffee. "I'll tell you where Indy is," she said. "Providing you answer a question for me."

"Anything, go ahead," Annabel said, immediately. She took another bite of the fluffy, delicious pastry.

"Did you mean it? What you said on the video?"

Her mouth was full and all she could do was nod furiously.

"You honestly, truly, with all your heart love her?" Lucinda said. "Because if you don't, you need to back off now. I'm not sure she can take being hurt. She made what she thought was a sensible decision to let you follow your career. You can't up-end that on a whim."

Annabel stared at the table, tears brewing in her eyes that she furiously blinked back. When she'd gathered herself, she spoke. "This isn't a whim," she said, fiercely. "I love her. More than anything."

Lucinda grinned. "In that case, I can tell you where she is. You'd better prepare yourself for this. She's, um, she's on a plane to California right now."

Annabel choked, needing two mouthfuls of steaming coffee to bring her back to her senses. "What?" she finally croaked.

"She's on a plane to California," Lucinda said, her eyes dancing with merriment.

"What on earth is she doing there?"

Lucinda laughed. "She's gone looking for you, of course."

And the world suddenly seemed like a lighter, better, more beautiful place. Because there was only one reason that Indy could be looking for her.

"Seriously?"

"Seriously," Lucinda said. "And you'd better have another coffee. Grab another of those pastries as well, my waist-line will thank you."

"No, no, I have to get going, I have to..." She had to what? What exactly was the next step here?

"You have to sit right there and finish your breakfast," Lucinda said. "Her plane isn't landing for another hour so you can't do a thing until then. And she'll call me as soon as she lands and then you can speak to her, alright?"

Annabel nodded numbly.

IT WAS more like two hours before Indy finally called and Lucinda let Annabel pick up the phone and the very first thing that Indy said was "I'm here."

Annabel took a breath. "That's a shame," she said. "Because I'm right here in your kitchen."

There was stunned silence, then: "Annabel?"

"Listen to me carefully," Annabel said. She'd had plenty of time to think about this and plan. "Go to the United desk. There's a ticket waiting for you there. You're going to get on the next flight to Chicago."

"What about you?" Indy's voice sounded so far away.

"I'm just about to leave for the airport. I'll meet you there."

A short pause. "Why Chicago?"

Annabel laughed. "It's halfway between here and Palo Alto and I'm damned if I'm waiting any longer than I have to to see your face. Now go, get that ticket and get on that plane. I'll be waiting for you."

CHAPTER THIRTY FIVE

Indy scrambled off her plane so fast that she tripped over a man's suitcase in first class and had to yell apologies over her shoulder.

"Coming through, coming through!" she shouted as she pounded down the jetway.

She was lucky that she only had hand luggage. Well, there hadn't exactly been time for anything else. There hadn't been time for anything but jumping on a plane and then wondering if she was going to regret what she was doing.

Hearing Annabel on the phone had been enough to set her fears at rest. This was it. This was crazy and stupid and fast, but she didn't care. She was ejected into the airport itself. She turned in circles, trying desperately to find the face she was looking for.

Nothing.

No one familiar.

The airport was crowded, maybe she'd missed her? Maybe she wasn't even here yet. Her stomach felt like ice. She'd waited so long, she couldn't stand to be disappointed now. A series of screens clung to the ceiling like a spider and she hurried over to them, scanning down, searching for any flight that Annabel might have been on.

"Hello."

And she froze.

Dead still.

She closed her eyes. If she turned now it would break the moment and she wanted to treasure this forever because she was finally, absolutely and completely sure that this was the start of something. The start of the whole rest of her life.

A hand descended on her shoulder, a flood of warmth coming off it, flowing down through her skin, tingling along nerves, tickling into every fiber of her being.

"Hello," the voice said again.

This time she did turn. She turned and Annabel was there and her face was beautiful and perfect and flawed all at once. Her eyes were dark and deep and every word that Indy had ever known flitted out of her head like so many butterflies.

But she didn't need words.

It was only a tiny step, but it seemed to take eons. Centuries passed as she moved closer and closer to Annabel's lips. Decades went by as she let her hands cup Annabel's soft face. Years crept on until she finally, finally touched her lips to Annabel's and the world stopped turning and nothing else mattered.

She disappeared into Annabel's kiss. Tasted the minty freshness of her gum, felt the pressure as Annabel's body pressed into her own, hipbones sliding against each other, fingers intertwining as they tried to make themselves into one single organism.

"It's them!"

The whispers shushed through her ears, then the words, then the clicking of phones and the flashes of light and only then did she start to hear what was really being said.

"It's #IndyAnna," someone said.

"No, it's—"

"Yes, it is, look!"

And Annabel was pushing away, grabbing her hand, leading her through the growing crowd of people.

"Vultures," she said.

Indy laughed. "You declared your love for me in front of the whole world, what did you expect?"

Annabel flushed a little. "It was an accident. I hit the wrong button, I meant to send it as a private message and, well, now all this."

Which just made Indy laugh harder. "You know, it's lucky it happened. I'm terrible with social media, I'd probably never have checked your message."

"You're not mad?"

"Mad about the most romantic, beautiful thing anyone has ever said to me? Are you crazy?"

Annabel growled and pulled her in closer, still walking, still moving away from people.

"I need to sit down," Indy protested. "My legs are still wobbly from that kiss."

"Over here," Annabel said, pointing to a small, dark bar in the corner of the airport.

Indy settled at a tiny table in the corner, her eyes on Annabel as she ordered drinks at the bar. She was afraid to look away. Afraid that Annabel would disappear or the world would change if she did.

She was bursting with the words now. She could hardly wait to say them. Annabel precariously balanced two full glasses of ice water and had barely placed them on the table when Indy spoke.

"I love you. I love you too. I was an idiot for never saying it before, I was a fool for thinking we could ignore all this, I'm so sorry. It took you, your courage, to push me into realizing that I've been an absolute, complete... silly-head."

"Silly-head?" Annabel said, sliding onto the bench seat next to her.

"Well, I'd already called myself an idiot and a fool, I couldn't think of anything else."

Annabel nodded gravely. "I meant everything that I said. Every word. I was wrong about so much, Indy. Wrong to think that romance didn't matter, wrong to think that I was better alone. I'm better with you. I want to be with you."

Indy shook her head. "It's been dark without you," she confessed. "I've been recording at the studio and the producer keeps complaining that I'm not energetic enough, that my music is different. It's because of you, I know that now."

"You know, I think we should have learned by now that ignoring things isn't the best plan. We ignored all the things that we thought were wrong about our relationship just so we could start something. And then..." Annabel looked at her thoughtfully. "And then when that doesn't work, we break things off, thinking that we'll just ignore our feelings instead."

"So we're both silly-heads, is that what you're saying?"

Annabel leaned in and brushed her lips against Indy's and Indy felt a tremor run down her spine.

"Both silly-heads, yes," whispered Annabel. But she drew back again. "And we're not making the same mistakes twice. We hash this out right here and right now. We want to make this work, so how are we going to do it? No more ignoring things in the hopes that they go away."

Blackness yawned in front of Indy again, a swirling hopelessness in her stomach. She knew what she had to do, and she knew that she'd do it, for Annabel there was nothing that she wouldn't do. "I, uh, I'll come to California. I'll call the production company in the morning. There are tons of studios in California, I'm sure that I'll get another chance out there."

Annabel shook her head. "No, there's no way I'm letting you do that."

Indy frowned. "But that's your dream, your amazing new job, I can't take that from you, you can't stay in the city just for me, *I* won't let *you* do that."

"Hold on, hold on," Annabel said, raising her hand and smiling. "I've had a lot of time to think about this, flying half-way across the country trying to catch up with you. What was all that about, by the way? Just jumping on a plane to Palo Alto hoping that you'd run into me on the street?"

"It was kind of impulsive," Indy said. "I'm not denying that. I just couldn't do nothing though, I couldn't watch that video and then not at least try to make a romantic gesture of my own."

"Ah-ha. I think we're going to have to have a conversation about romantic gestures at some point," Annabel said. "But for now, the practicalities. Indy, I would give up California for you, if that was my only choice, I absolutely would. And I know you'd give up the city for me. But what if we didn't have to? What if we could compromise at least a little?"

The yawning blackness was receding. "I'm listening."

"Alright, you keep your place in the city, keep paying rent, go to the studio when you need to, etc. etc. I get a new place in California and start my new job. And then, well, then we keep on flying across the country."

"We cross the country every time we want to see each other?"

"Hey, if it's stupid and it works, it's not stupid. I can negotiate telecommuting for one day a week, you won't need to be in the studio all the time, with a little bit of work we can make this happen, Indy. All we have to do is want it enough."

Indy was already settling into the idea. "I guess it could work."

"We can try," Annabel said. She took Indy's hands. "There are no guarantees in life, I know that. And maybe it won't work, maybe we won't work, I don't know the future. I do know that I love you. And that I want to try everything in my power to make sure that we're both as happy as we can be."

Indy was nodding. "Yes, yes, okay, I see it, I see how we could do this."

"Six months," Annabel said. "We'll do it for six months and if we're not happy we'll re-evaluate. Maybe one of us will really want to move then, or maybe this relationship won't be going in the direction we think it should. We don't have to do this for the rest of our lives."

But Indy was barely listening now. She was edging in, watching the plumpness of Annabel's lips as she spoke. "What if I want to do this for the rest of my life?"

"Want to do what?" Annabel asked, voice hoarse.

"This," Indy said, pushing into the kiss again, letting it wash over her, letting her nerve-endings spark and her heart take flight.

Annabel had to push her away. "Come on."

"Where are we going?"

"We have a flight to catch."

"We do?" Indy asked, letting herself be pulled up from the table.

"I need to get you home," said Annabel, pulling her into yet another kiss. "Because if I don't, I'm about to do very, very naughty things on a plane and I don't think I should risk my frequent flier status, not with all the traveling we're planning on doing."

Indy laughed and let herself be pulled along.

They were half-way to the ticketing desk when Annabel's phone rang. She took the call, stepping to the side so that Indy couldn't hear the conversation. When she came back, she had a slightly worried look on her face.

"That was Laura," she said.

"And?"

"And the new owners of LBN weren't especially pleased with my little video. At least at first. But then they saw #IndyAnna trending and their subscriber base starting to grow yet again and, well, they've mostly decided to forgive me."

"Mostly?" Indy asked, heart thrumming.

"They like the publicity," said Annabel. "Like it so much that we're encouraged to court it, and in return they'll forget about my little mishap."

Indy looked around and could see several people looking at them, one holding up a phone as he filmed them. And then she laughed, clasping Annabel's arm in her own. "Oh well, I guess we'd better give them something to look at to keep you out of jail," she said as she stood on tiptoes to kiss Annabel's cheek.

"Hey, no one said anything about jail!"

Indy rolled her eyes. "We're going to have to work on that teasing thing, too," she said.

And Annabel laughed as they walked arm in arm through the airport to buy a ticket home.

EPILOGUE

The bar was buzzing and the guests were chattering and Indy was drinking. Not a lot, but enough to try and get up the courage that she needed to have the conversation she needed to have.

"Woah, slow down there, soldier," Lucinda said, joining her at the bar. "What's the hurry?"

Indy took another drink. "Dutch courage."

"You still haven't told her?" Lucinda asked, laughing. "Jesus, you two. I swear, this relationship would move faster if you just sent each other smoke signals across the country."

"I'm working on it," Indy said. Although she knew that she was actually procrastinating. It wasn't that she didn't want to do this, she did. It was just that she didn't know how Annabel was going to react.

"Nice baptism," Lucinda said. "Not that I've actually been to one before."

"Neither have I," said Indy. "But it was nice to be invited anyway."

"You're the partner of the godmother, I don't think Billy and Cassie had much choice on that," Lucinda said, getting herself a drink. "I, on the other hand, am honored to be invited. Though Cassie and I have been hanging out a whole bunch with you and Annabel being in and out of town."

"Good," said Indy. "I'm glad you're making new friends." She looked at her glass. "I, uh, I'm sorry if I'm leaving you in the lurch with the apartment and everything."

"Not at all." Lucinda leaned on the bar. "First up, as of next week I'll officially be a real lawyer working at a law firm and everything. And secondly, well, there's someone that I was thinking about maybe asking to possibly, perhaps move in. Maybe."

Indy raised her eyebrows. "Evelyn?"

"Yes," said Lucinda. "Only I haven't asked her yet, and I'm not sure what she's going to say."

"And you're on my case about being slow," Indy said. "Seriously, the girl is mad about you. She's been dying to move things on to the next stage but didn't want to bother you while you were busy taking the bar and all."

"Seriously?" Lucinda said. "In that case, I guess I should ask her." She turned around and managed to catch Evelyn's eye at a table a few feet away. "Hey, Evie?"

"Yeah?"

"Want to move in with me?"

Indy watched in awe as Evelyn's face smoothed out and a smile beamed.

"Sure thing, Luce."

Lucinda turned back to Indy, a huge grin on her face. "See, it's that easy. You should probably go find Annabel now, don't you think?"

* * *

"Ugh," said Cassie, carefully pulling out a seat next to Annabel. "My arms are killing me. Here, you hold her for a second."

Much against Annabel's initial expectations, she found that she quite liked holding Yasmin. The baby was adorable with her dark hair and darker skin, her eyes like liquid chocolate as they took everything in. She was small and perfect and Annabel had a strange urge to want to protect her.

"Billy's having the time of his life," she said as Cassie stretched her legs out.

"He's relieved that the adoption actually went through," said Cassie. "This has been hard on him."

"Hard on you too."

"No," Cassie said, shaking her head. "Billy's the one that had to learn that he wasn't broken, that he wasn't a failure just because he couldn't biologically father a child. That had nothing to do with me. I'm just glad that I've got my husband back and he can smile again." She grunted. "And that he's willing to do the two a.m. feed."

Annabel laughed.

"What about you?" Cassie said. "Any chance we should expect the patter of tiny feet coming from your direction any time soon? Or is that off the cards?"

Annabel shook her head. "I don't know," she said, honestly. "I just... I don't know where this is going. It's been eighteen months and we're still skipping back and forth across the country all the time and nothing has changed. I think maybe we're both afraid to change. Or maybe Indy's happy with the way things are. I don't know."

"But you're not happy?"

Annabel smiled down at Yasmin who was sleeping contentedly. "Strangely enough, no, I don't think I am. I'd never have thought it but... But I'm ready to move on, I'm ready to make this real, to, I don't know, at least live in the same time zone. But Indy... I'm not sure what she wants."

"There's only one way to find out," Cassie said. "You need to talk to her."

"But what if she doesn't want to change?"

"Then the two of you need to figure out a way for you both to be happy. Ignoring things in the hope that they go away is not a psychologist-recommended way to conduct a relationship."

"I know, I know," Annabel said. "We need to talk. I've been putting it off for too long."

"Want me to take her back?" Cassie said, tucking a blanket

neatly around Yasmin's chin.

"No," Annabel said. "Let me keep her for just a few minutes more. Why don't you get yourself a drink?"

※ ※ ※

The party was starting to wind down and Indy knew that she'd been avoiding Annabel, and she knew that that was stupid. If nothing else, she shouldn't waste the precious amount of time they had together by being cowardly.

She finally ordered two whiskeys and found Annabel sitting at a table checking her phone.

"And here was me thinking that you were avoiding me," Annabel said, grinning as she took the drink.

"I might have been," Indy admitted. She could see a sheen of paleness pass over Annabel's face.

"And why would that be?" Annabel asked, keeping her tone light.

Indy sighed and sipped at her drink. "There's something we need to talk about. Actually, there's something that I need to say, to tell you. And I've been putting it off because I didn't know how you were going to react, and, well, because I didn't want to spoil one of our lovely weekends together by potentially arguing over something."

Annabel nodded. She was quiet, not looking Indy in the eye and Indy knew that she was dreading something, knew that she was afraid.

"I love you," she said, trying to take some of the fear away.

"You love me," Annabel said. "But... I feel like there's a 'but' coming along here."

"But I feel like we've gotten too comfortable with the situation that we're in," said Indy. "And this isn't what I want, it's never what I've wanted."

Annabel cleared her throat. "Okay. Okay, I can see that." She looked away again, blinking, and Indy could see that there were tears there.

She didn't want Annabel to cry. She didn't want Annabel to hurt. But she didn't know if what she was going to say was going to make things better or worse. Either way, she needed to spit it out and put them both out of their misery.

"I've got an offer to work in a studio in San Francisco," she said as quickly as she could. "It would mean moving full time to California."

Now Annabel was looking at her and her mouth was wide open and the tears were gone and Indy was terrified that she'd said the wrong thing.

"I, uh, I don't have to live with you," she added quickly. "I can get my own place, I just thought—"

"You don't have to live with me," Annabel interrupted. "But I want you to live with me."

Indy sunk the rest of her drink so fast she felt it burning in her throat. "Are you serious?"

"Deadly," said Annabel. "I've been wanting to say something for ages, but I was afraid that you'd think I was coming on too strong, that you wouldn't want to move in with me, or you wouldn't want me to come back to the city, or..."

"So we both ignored the issue," Indy finished. She shook her head. "We really need to stop doing that."

Annabel took her hand. "We do," she said.

They sat for a while, hand in hand, watching Billy cradle Yasmin in his arms as Cassie kissed guests goodbye.

"I've been thinking," Indy said. "I think it's time to retire the bucket list."

"Really?" Annabel said. "But then how will you know what you have left to do in life?"

Indy grinned. "Actually, I was thinking that maybe it was time to make a new one. Together. A joint list."

"Okay," said Annabel, still watching Billy. "We could put moving in together on the list."

"We could," agreed Indy. "And maybe we could put getting married on the list. You know, for one day, later." Her heart beat fast as she said it.

"We could," Annabel said. "Perhaps we could think about putting something else on the list too?" She darted a glance at Indy, then looked again at Billy.

"A baby, maybe?" Indy suggested, her heart filling up so full that she was surprised it worked at all.

"We could," said Annabel. "You know, for later. When we've talked about it and agreed."

Indy nodded. "I think there are a lot of things we could put on our list."

They weren't perfect. Indy knew that they never would be. And that was just fine with her. It was their differences and flaws that made them interesting, that made them unique, like flakes of snow or grains of sand.

They never would be perfect. Despite all their best intentions, she knew that every now and again they'd slip, and ignore something that shouldn't be ignored until one of them came to their senses. And that was just fine.

It was fine because, no matter what, they would be together.

She stood up, holding out her hand. "Shall we go home?"

Annabel took it. "I think we should."

Indy led them out, flagging down a cab when they got to the street. Because the only thing she wanted was to curl up in Annabel's arms and start planning their bucket list. A list of possibilities. A list of landmarks and events and actions that would define them as a couple. A list that they could look back on when they were old and sitting on the porch.

"What do you think about a nickname?" Indy asked, as they got into the cab. "Annabel is a bit of a mouthful."

"I think it's something we could discuss," Annabel said. "As long as you're willing to discuss me calling you Indigo."

Indy shivered and cuddled in closer to Annabel. "If we can't even decide what to call each other, how are we going to name a child?"

"We'll put up a survey on the internet," said Annabel crisply. "Or I could design an algorithm to come up with the perfect name."

"You can't choose a name with an algorithm."

Annabel looked down at her and grinned. "An algorithm chose me and you."

"Fair point," said Indy. "I suppose you'd better start programming it then."

And the cab turned a corner and they were pressed together and Indy could see the whole wide future spreading out in front of them.

THANKS FOR READING!

If you liked this book, why not leave a review? Reviews are so important to independent authors, they help new readers discover us, and give us valuable feedback. Every review is very much appreciated.

And if you want to stay up to date with the latest Sienna Waters news and new releases, then follow me on Twitter or on Facebook!
Keep reading for a sneak peek of my next book!

BOOKS FROM SIENNA WATERS

The Oakview Series:

Coffee For Two
Saving the World
Rescue My Heart
Dance With Me
Learn to Love
Away from Home
Picture Me Perfect

The Monday's Child Series:

Fair of Face
Full of Grace
Full of Woe

The Hawkin Island Series:

More than Me

Standalone Books:

The Opposite of You
French Press
The Wrong Date
Everything We Never Wanted
Fair Trade
One For The Road
The Real Story
A Big Straight Wedding
A Perfect Mess
Love By Numbers
Ready, Set, Bake

Or turn the page to get a sneak preview of Ready, Set, Bake!

READY, SET, BAKE

Chapter One

A bead of sweat trickled from her hairline and very slowly began to inch its way down her nose until it reached the end and hesitated. Joey gritted her teeth determined not to wipe it away.

The problem with yoga was that no matter what happened, everything else was so slow that even something as tiny as a drop of sweat was enough to grab her attention and hold it. She tensed her muscles and held her pose and the drip finally, inevitably, fell to the ground and she felt like cheering for the little guy, but she kept her mouth shut.

She brought her hands up and shifted her balance, following the instructor exactly. The instructor that had such great pants. Yellow and blue and exactly the right cut and where on earth did she get them? There was that sporting goods store at the end of the block, maybe that...

Focus.

Breathe in, breathe out.

She picked her foot up, moving her balance yet again. The woman in front of her wobbled. She had nice hair, thick and bouncy, the color like that of old rust, deep and beautiful. Was the color natural? And what about the curl, surely that wasn't real, it must have taken hours with a curler if it wasn't, and who had that kind of time before a yoga class?

Focus.

Just for a couple more minutes. Hold it together.

Bending her body over she could feel the pull of a muscle. So she must be doing something right. To be perfectly honest, she'd doubted that yoga was particularly good exercise. Like, how could sitting with your legs crossed cancel out all those cake calories? Another bead of sweat ran from her hairline, diverting around her nose this time.

Yeah. Yoga wasn't quite as easy as she'd thought. Which was fine. At least she'd tried it, right? Which was the most important thing. Though the chances of her being on her death bed and being glad that she'd bothered to take a yoga class were slim. Still, you never knew. Better to cover all bases and have no regrets.

"And exhale."

Joey stood up, her blonde hair flipping back into place as the instructor with the fabulous pants beamed at the room.

"Excellent, great class, guys, well done." She spread her arms wide like she wanted to hug the whole room and Joey felt a minuscule beat of pride.

She'd done it. Survived the yoga class. Not that she was planning on coming back. This wasn't for her, she was pretty certain about that.

"Is it always like this?" she inquired of the woman next to her as they both bent to roll up their mats.

"Like what?" the woman asked.

"Um, so... slow?" Joey tried.

The woman grinned. "Yep. That's kind of the thing with yoga, mindfulness and all that."

"Jeez." Joey scratched her nose, remembering the feel of the drip of sweat running down it.

"You like things a little more high-octane then?" asked the woman as they stood in line to return their mats.

"Yes," Joey said. Then: "No." Then: "Maybe?"

The woman laughed and there was a slight gap between her

front teeth that made her look more approachable even though Joey had imagined that she was a cold-hearted banker. Mostly because her hair was in a french twist.

"Well, maybe you should try something else then?" she suggested. "Like kite surfing, for example."

"What's that?" Joey stacked her mat and followed the other woman toward the changing rooms.

"As far as I understand it, you strap yourself to a big old kite and then tie your feet to a surfboard and off you go, skimming the tops of the waves," the woman said. "At least that's the idea. Or, you know, you could try heli-skiing."

"Please tell me that doesn't involve strapping myself to a helicopter."

The woman laughed. "No, it involves being dropped out of a helicopter onto virgin ski runs. It's pretty dangerous and totally expensive."

Huh. She did like skiing. Heli-skiing. It might be something to look into. Something to try. And kite-surfing didn't sound that bad either. Both of those could be something that she'd regret not trying. Both of them could be things that on her death bed she could honestly say she was glad she'd done. Or, you know, either one could put her on her death bed.

"Gotta run," the woman said, cramming her sweatshirt into her bag. "I've got a meeting."

"Oh, at the bank," Joey said, completely forgetting that the woman hadn't told her she was a banker at all and it was all in her imagination.

The woman frowned. "No, uh, with a client. I'm an architect."

"Oh," was all Joey could say and the woman half-smiled at her and then scooted off.

Which was the problem with making up scenarios in her head. Sometimes she forgot that they just weren't real. Slowly, she pulled off her sweaty socks and slung them into her bag, sliding her bare feet into street sneakers. Time to head home for a shower.

She paused at the big noticeboard in the lobby, checking out the ads for new classes, looking for something else to try. Zumba she'd already done, yoga was checked off the list, spinning was so old school, hmmm, kick-boxing, that might be fun.

For a second she tried to imagine kick-boxing Ross in the face. Or one of his many, many girlfriends. She sighed. She just wasn't violent enough for that. Try as she might, her imagination drew the line right before her foot connected with anyone else and the imagined picture petered out.

Still though, kick-boxing could be cool.

She stopped at the front desk and signed up for a trial class before she left.

"Yoga not for you, huh?" grinned the regular guy behind the desk.

"Nope." Then she got worried. "Is there like a limit to the number of trial classes I can take?"

He shrugged. "Not as far as I know. You're free to try things out until you find what's right for you. And you're all signed up, Mrs. McGinnis."

"Ms."

He blushed. "Ms. My apologies, ma'am."

She left the building a lot less calm than she'd have thought, just having finished a yoga class and all. Ma'am? Really? She was thirty two. Surely she didn't deserve a ma'am yet?

She was debating whether or not 'ma'am' would warrant being kick-boxed in the face when her phone started vibrating in her bag. She hustled to get it out before the ringing stopped.

"Joe, is that you?"

"Who else would be answering my phone?"

"With the way you are these days, I have no idea."

Joey rolled her eyes but said nothing. Kate was her best friend which gave her a certain lee-way to criticize. Besides, she sounded flustered and out of sorts.

"Listen, Joe, have you got a half hour or so? Like around now would be good."

Joey looked down at her sweaty gym clothes. "Um, not really. I mean, I can be with you in an hour or so but I really gotta run home first and—"

"Please? It's important."

"Then tell me over the phone," Joey said, jogging across the street and raising a hand at the cab-driver that had let her cross.

"No, this is something really best done in person."

"And it can't wait like, forty five minutes?" Enough time to shower but not wash her hair.

"I'll buy you cake."

Cake. Okay, that sounded better. But still, she must stink. "Kate, I just need to grab a shower."

"Come on, nobody cares. Anyway, won't the cake taste better with the sweat still sticking to your skin? Like a glorious reward?"

Joey laughed and Kate pressed her point.

"And how often do we get to goof off and eat cake in the middle of the day?"

"Never."

"Exactly," Kate said. "Carpe diem and all that."

Joey rubbed a hand across her shiny forehead. Carpe diem. And it wasn't exactly like Ross was sitting at home waiting for her. There was nobody sitting at home waiting for her.

"It's important, isn't it?"

There was a crackling silence and then Kate said: "I wouldn't ask otherwise. I really need you, Joe. Please come."

Kate rarely asked for anything. She was independent, strong-willed and more than capable of looking after herself. Joey, on the other hand, had collapsed like a stringless puppet the moment that Ross had left and had called on Kate more than once to help her put her life back together again. So she owed her. Big time.

And there was cake.

"Yeah, of course I'll come." The shower could wait. "Where are you at?"

Kate reeled off an address that was close to her office and Joey told her to hang tight and she'd be there ASAP.

What could be so important that Kate of all people, responsible Kate, was willing to take off in the middle of the work-day? She skipped a couple of steps and then started to hurry her way through the streets. Her interest was perked. And her stomach was rumbling. All that yoga was much more hard work than she'd expected. A nice slice of cake was just what she needed.

CHAPTER TWO

The whiny strains of the theme from Love Story echoed through the empty shop. Sophia bit her lip to stop herself yelling at her sister and bent her head back over the papers she was working with.

Whether she could concentrate or not made little difference at this point. She knew the numbers. She sighed. If, and only if, she could persuade the coffee shop on the corner to pay their bill in full by the end of the week, then they'd just about make rent on the shop. She'd shaved as much off costs as she could.

Or had she?

She bent down again and looked at her supplier list. Laura's whistling got louder.

"For God's sake!"

Sophia threw down her pen and Laura looked up from her piping work. An elegant looking cupcake sat on the stand in front of her, half-decorated with curls of pale pink buttercream. "What?" she asked innocently.

"Can you change the tune?" Sophia asked. "Or better yet, stop the whistling altogether?"

"It helps me concentrate," Laura said. But she picked up her piping bag again and started to work silently.

Cutting supplier costs meant accepting lower-quality products which, in the long run, probably wasn't the best idea. The shop had a reputation, after all. Okay, not the kind of reputation that let her charge twenty bucks per cupcake, but still.

Laura started to hum the theme from Love Story under her breath.

"Laur, I'll put that piping nozzle up your nose."

"Sorry, sorry."

She scowled down at the paperwork, willing something to change and then giving up when it didn't. She started piling the papers together, they made less of an impact when they were in a neat stack as opposed to spread out over the table. Laura started humming.

"Laura!"

Her sister laid down her piping bag and beamed. "Done," she said. "What do you think?" She carried the stand over and placed it in front of Sophia.

"Nice," Sophia said, nodding begrudgingly.

"Taste test." Laura pulled out a knife and neatly sliced the cake in half.

Sophia regarded it critically for a second, noting the crumb, the level of moisture, and finding nothing she could complain about she took a mouthful. "Not bad. Could use a hint more salt and maybe a pinch less of the lavender."

Her sister licked her fingers. "I think it's perfect. And I think you're little miss cranky pants. What's up?"

"Nothing."

"Bullshit."

Laura's eyebrows were perfect arches and Sophia didn't know how she managed to keep them looking so perfect. Her sister was lax in pretty much everything except cake decoration and eyebrow management. Sharing a room growing up had meant drawing a literal line down the middle and letting Laura keep her mess on one side whilst her own side stayed meticulously neat.

"I was trying to work," Sophia said.

"So was I," pouted Laura.

"I was trying to make sense of the numbers from our failing business."

"And I was trying to make a product that our business can sell," Laura said, tossing her dark hair over her shoulder. "And we're not dead yet. It's not over until it's over so stop being overdramatic. We're not a failed business."

"That's not how language works. The presence of the -ing in 'failing' denotes that something is in the process of happening, which is important if you want to stop that thing happening and prevent the addition of the -ed on the end of the verb, which denotes that something is over and done with."

"Jesus, Sophia, lighten up." Laura peered more closely at her and Sophia shuffled uncomfortably. "What the hell is wrong? You're cranky even for you."

"Nothing."

"Tell me or I'll give you a dead arm."

Sophia sighed again. Laura was allegedly thirty one. The only reason she could believe that was because she'd been there for all thirty one of those years. The girl acted like she was eight most of the time.

Just as she was about to say 'nothing' again, Laura reached for her arm and Sophia hurriedly pulled away.

"Fine. I signed the divorce papers this morning, happy?"

"Wow." Laura pulled back immediately. "Wow. I'm sorry, Soph. I had no idea. I... I'm sorry."

"Don't be. It needed doing and now it's done." Which should be the motto of her life, Sophia thought.

"No, you're allowed to feel something. You don't have to be so... so stiff-upper-lip about it. I'm really sorry, Soph. Truly I am. That must have been a hell of a morning. You should have taken the day off."

A hell of a morning. It was nothing compared to that night a year ago when she'd come home late from the shop and the apartment had echoed empty. Emptier than usual. Sure, the furniture was still there, the clutter of shoes by the door, the unopened junkmail on the side table. But there'd been something wrong, she'd known it as soon as she'd walked through the door.

It had taken a while to figure out what exactly was going on since Jenna hadn't bothered to leave a note. Not that it should have come as such a huge surprise. They'd been drifting apart for months, like two boats on the ocean. Until Jenna had decided to rev up her motor and rocket off completely over the horizon.

"I don't have time to take a day off. There are things that need doing around here."

"What's the point of owning your own business if you don't get to skip work every now and again?" Laura said.

She'd reached out and put her hand over Sophia's and Sophia hated herself for wanting the contact. For wanting any contact. It was better that she and Jenna were apart, she'd accepted that now. But her life was so much lonelier.

"Owning a failing business, remember?"

Laura grunted and sat back in her chair. "You can't carry the weight of the world on your shoulders, you know?"

"Says the person who just the other day called me to come over and catch a spider in her bath-tub."

"It was hairy."

"I was sleeping."

Laura flashed her a small grin. "But you did it anyway because you're my big sister and I love you."

She'd done it because that was what she did. She did stuff. Stuff that no one else wanted to do. Stuff that had to be done.

"We're not really doing that badly, are we?" Laura asked now.

And her big, blue eyes were wide and scared and Sophia couldn't bring herself to tell the real truth. The whole truth.

Laura had been twelve years old when their father had left. He'd just gone to work one morning and not come back. They'd never heard from him again. For a while, they'd entertained ideas that he had amnesia, or that he'd been kidnapped and held hostage. Well, Laura had entertained those ideas. She watched a lot of soap operas.

But Sophia had heard their mother crying late at night. At sixteen, she had a much better idea of what was going on. Her heart had broken but she'd been paralyzed with the enormity of what had happened to their family. Dad was the bread-winner, the sole provider.

Then one night, Laura had crawled into her bed and sobbed and said that she knew dad wasn't coming back and that he'd run away to live with someone else and she'd sounded like her world was falling apart.

So Sophia had shaken off the paralysis and done what she had to.

She'd baked.

Figuring that if she could sell cakes at school bake sales then she could sell cakes anywhere, she'd started baking night and day, using up every hour that she wasn't in school, selling cupcakes at break time and cakes at baseball games and small graduation and engagement cakes and gradually, slowly building up a business.

Between the cakes and welfare and their mom's disability checks they'd made it. Sophia had graduated high school and educated herself the rest of the way using books and the internet. She'd made sure that Laura stayed in school and even gone to community college. She'd supported the family.

She still supported the family.

Laura worked full time in the shop and Sophia made sure that ma's rent was paid and that there were groceries in the refrigerator when she went over there once a week.

She was planning on giving up her own apartment. Now that the divorce was real there was no point having the extra expense. She'd move back in with ma, all the better to take care of her. The extra money could go into the business. As long as the business could survive the next six months until her lease was up.

"Soph?"

"Yeah?"

"We're not in such bad shape, are we?"

Sophia sighed. They were. But she shrugged. "It's nothing for you to worry about. I'll take care of it."

And Laura smiled again and that really was all that was important. Keep her family happy, keep things ticking over, and now all she needed to do was win the lottery. Or start selling her body. She wondered just how much an escort on the wrong side of thirty was charging these days.

"I know you will," Laura said. "You always take care of everything." She stood up and brushed a kiss on Sophia's cheek. "And now I'm heading out of here, unless you want some help cleaning up and closing?"

Sophia shook her head. "Nah, I got it. Off you go."

The whistling started again as Laura went off to get her coat and bag, leaving the cake stand and dirty knife sitting on the table. Sophia waited until her sister was gone before she picked the items up and took them to the industrial sink in the back.

Get Your Copy of Ready, Set, Bake Now!

Printed in Great Britain
by Amazon